THE VINEGAROON MURDERS

VOLUME TWO

OF THE DOS CRUCES TRILOGY

THE VINEGAROON MURDERS

by

JAMES A. MANGUM

JOHN M. HARDY PUBLISHING

ALPINE & HOUSTON

2006

First Printing: March 2006

1 3 5 7 9 8 6 4 2

ISBN 0-9717667-7-0

Printed and Bound in the United States of America

Jacket design — Leisha Israel, Digital Tractor

Cover photograph — Bryan Reynolds

John M. Hardy Publishing Company
Houston, Texas

www.johnmhardy.com

To Sid...thanks for everything.

Acknowledgments

Special thanks to: Jeremy, for your valuable input; Jamie, Jill and Jodie, for your moral support; Dave, for your forthrightness; Sylvia, Kathy, and Jesús for your translation help; Kyle, for your many edits; Leisha, for your beautiful covers; Mike, for being a good publisher and a good friend; John and Myrna, for being there.

And the Lord said to Raphael: "Bind Azazel hand and foot, and cast him into the darkness; and make an opening in the desert, which is in Dudael, and cast him therein. And place upon him rough and jagged rocks, and cover him with darkness, and let him abide there forever."

– *The Book of Enoch*

Contents

PART III

The Investigation

PART IV

The Judgment

THE VINEGAROON MURDERS

Prologue

Standing on Jamey Maxwell's tiny porch of his tiny house in the tiny town of Dos Cruces, Texas, Sheriff Arlen Buckner says, "I know you killed those men. And I know Mari was involved somehow. I also know I cannot prove any of this.

"For some reason, I don't blame you for her death. I think she loved you, but God only knows why. I could hate you, but don't want to spend that much energy on you. I have no interest in pursuing this case any further. Those men deserved to die. But do not make the mistake of crossing my path again...ever. Get my fucking drift, Maxwell?"

Jamey Maxwell just nods. Arlen Buckner turns, steps down from the tiny porch at St. Charles Place, gets in his patrol car and drives away.

Part I

The Meek

(They Shall Inherit...blah, blah, blah...)

Chapter 1

The Santero

Her eyes half-closed; her lips slightly parted; the look of pure ecstasy. How long has it been? How long has he worked for this? How many times has he run his hands up and down her flawlessly smooth body? That look of rapture. So perfect, so peaceful, so permanent. *La Virgen de Guadalupe*: the carving is finished at last.

Chapter 2

The Sheepherder

Manuelito smells death. *Muerte.* Although he is only seventeen, it is a smell that has become all too familiar in his life. And death has come to him in many forms: coyotes, an occasional golden eagle, on rare occasions wild hogs, but more often than not, dogs. Packs of semi-wild dogs. They are a sheepherder's worst enemy. During the last eight years of Manuelito's watch, they have killed hundreds of his sheep. Dawn is breaking and the smell of death is in the air. But today it is different. And as yet unseen. It is May 15.

By nine o'clock, with the West Texas heat already building, Manuelito discovers the two bodies. A man and a woman, entwined in a death embrace amongst the rocks. They are covered with vinegaroons. Manuelito calls the vinegaroons *alacranes del diablo.* Devil scorpions. Although he has walked the forty-square mile Galvan Ranch thousands of times over the last eight years, he has seen a vinegaroon only twice before. And only at night. Now he sees dozens of them scurrying over the dead couple, pinchers gnashing and whiptails thrashing. Here in the light of day, they are frantically searching for something.

Manuelito mumbles, "*Dios sabe lo que hace,*" makes the sign of the cross and starts to cry.

Chapter 3

The Sheep

Daniel, the goatboy, is walking the red dirt streets of Dos Cruces. He is smiling, as always. He is thinking about his new baby goat. If Daniel had religion, the baby goat would be Baby Jesus. He worships the little one.

Daniel is on his way to the *santero's* workshop. Taz, the wonderdog, is leading the way, as always. This has been their daily routine for some time now. Ever since Jamey Maxwell became Miguel Veras' — the *santero's* — apprentice. This has made Daniel even happier. This has made Taz, Miguel Veras, and Jamey Maxwell less sad. *Da lo mismo.*

Evil is close to Daniel now. It brushes his shoulder, blows in his ear. Daniel is oblivious to it, though. This makes Evil crazy. This makes Evil mean. Evil hates Daniel. *Pero, Dios no les dio alas a los alacranes.* God did not give wings to scorpions. Or did He?

Taz has his left ear cocked, nose in the air. Taz is aware.

Part II

The Murders

Chapter 1

The Seraph

Jamey Maxwell is dreaming of angels. Seraphim, Cherubim, Thrones, and Dominions. And, of course, the Fallen Ones. He recognizes almost every face. His sweet Josie. Julie, so beautiful. Connie Lee, but...where are her eyes? Luther and Dwayne. No Chango though. Marisol smiles at him, but she's been crying. He wants to tell her it will be okay, but he is unable to speak. He awakes, choking.

The dreams — the nightmares — come every night now after a year of sweet respite. He fears working with the *santero* is not helping things. This is irrelevant of course, because God chooses to project these images into Jamey's dreams. You humans would call it brainwashing. And what Jamey is seeing is not actually Seraphim, Cherubim, etc. He could not survive that experience. He is seeing a diluted, sanitized, humanized version of angels. Something he can live to tell about, if he chooses to. I doubt that he will. Jamey no longer speaks of his conversations with God or of his visions. He wants to appear somewhat normal. He wants to live in the real world again. Fat chance.

How do I know all of this? Well, let's just say that I am one of God's messengers. A Watcher. An angel if you will. What theologians, especially Jewish theologians, would call a Seraph. But let me get this straight up front. Ancient Hebrew prophets, particularly Enoch, defined the nine choirs of the heavenly hierarchy and they were surprisingly accurate with one major and a few minor exceptions. Seraphim are not the highest order of angel. Oh no. Quite the opposite in fact. Here is the true ranking (at least as far as humans can understand it) from highest to lowest: Cherubim, Thrones, Dominions, Powers, Virtues, Principalities, Archangels, Angels, Seraphim. There you are. I'm at the bottom of the celestial food chain. For a human comparison, let's just say that my name is Shyanne and I live in a trailer park in Del Rio, Texas. And let's just say I work as a barmaid at the Come On Inn, Highway 90 West, on the outskirts of Del Rio. Just trying to give you something to wrap your mind around.

Several other things before we get on with this story. First, I will speak to you in the human vernacular. I love speaking human. I will use slang, I will use Tex-Mex, and I will use expletives. Lots of expletives. I like them...a lot. I will talk to you on your level. And you don't have a clue just how low that is. But we Seraphs love you anyway. I will speak to you of the big picture. I will speak to you of the small picture. The minutiae. I love the minutiae. With humans, it's where "the rubber meets the road." How's that for some human vernacular? I will speak to the trifles of your lives; the trifles that you, as God's creations, have inexplicably created for yourselves: love, hate, sex, murder, longing, desperation, religion, jealousy, greed. We can call all of this "An Angel Goes Slumming."

Second, at times you will perceive my thoughts and words to be contradictory. "Perceive" being the key word in that sentence. I suggest you read between the lines. Or not. *No le hace*. Who are you to judge contradictions, anyway? After all, your entire lives as humans...your *raisons d'etre*...are nothing but contradiction. In the art of contradiction, you are the masters. I, just a rank amateur.

Third, guardian angels exist, but not in the way humans imagine. You would not want to see them. Visualize every monster under the bed or in the closet when you were a child rolled into one and on steroids, acid, and crack cocaine. They are not really angels. They are a separate species. This is why they are not included in the nine choirs. What apes are to humans, guardian angels are to angels. They are dim-witted, irrational, unpredictable. They cannot tell the good guys from the bad guys. The universe would be better off without them, but what can I say? It's God's will. Don't bother trying to understand it.

And finally, speaking of God's will, there is only one mortal sin in God's eyes and it's not included in the Ten Commandments, Bible, Koran, Torah, or any of your so-called sacred writings. It's the one thing mankind has never gotten, to mankind's eternal detriment. The one mortal sin, the one that God never forgives, is presumptuousness. Specifically, presuming to know God's will. Because He doesn't always know it Himself. God does not like to be second-guessed. So, a little hint before we continue with this tale: if you have a bumper sticker on your vehicle that reads "In Case of Rapture, This Car Will Be Unmanned," I would suggest you invest, ASAP, in a razor blade scraper and remove said bumper sticker. And, oh yes, if you actually believe said bumper sticker, I would suggest you invest, ASAP, in a frontal lobotomy. Never forget this point. Now to the story.

Chapter 2

The Summons

As we Seraphs like to say, "Eternity's a bitch, and then it's not over."

Jamey Maxwell is dreaming again. He is at his seemingly perfect home in Houston with his beautiful Connie Lee and his precious daughters, Julie and Josie. They have been dead for years now. But this is what dreams are about, isn't it?

The four of them are sitting at the kitchen table. For some inexplicable reason, the kitchen table is in the living room now. The elegantly decorated living room, with Connie Lee's special touch. But Jamey senses there is something wrong; much like the "Can You Find What's Wrong with This Picture?" coloring books from his childhood. Some things in this room are out of place; some things in this room are out of focus. And although he cannot quite see them, Jamey also knows some things in this room are dead.

Josie is talking about her friend Allison. "Mom, she has a boyfriend now and she's acting so stuck up about it." Julie smiles her shy smile while looking down at the table. Connie Lee is looking at Josie and then at Jamey, to get his reaction. At first, she is smiling that smile he remembers so well. The one that always let him know he was the only man in her world. The conversation continues and Connie Lee's head begins to swivel back and forth between Josie and Jamey with the beat of a metronome. Now Jamey is inside a glass box, still sitting at the table. He is able to hear Josie's voice...but only hers. Her usually sweet voice is starting to rise; it's becoming harsh. Connie Lee's head pivots faster as Josie talks louder. Julie's shy smile becomes wider. Jamey can see her braces. Josie is talking discordantly, "And Veronica is a slut!"

Water begins to rise inside the glass box. Josie begins to screech in disjointed phrases. Jamey can make out fewer and fewer words. He realizes Josie is now talking in tongues. But she punctuates the religious babble with the vilest of obscenities. Connie Lee's swiveling head is now a blur.

The water continues to rise. It is now up to Jamey's chest. Julie's smile has grown so wide her face is beginning to distort. She is no longer wearing braces. And the teeth are perfectly straight. They are not her teeth though. They do not belong in the mouth of a sweet, shy teenage girl. They belong in the mouth of a small but vicious fish found in the jungles of the Amazon. They belong in the mouth of a piranha.

Josie's raging voice is spewing forth the most disgusting profanities. This from his thirteen-year-old daughter who has never cursed in her life. "Debbie is a fat fucking dickeating whore! *Basilica domini Yahweh entradum!* Monica is a cocksucking cuntlicker!" With the piranha teeth, Julie is now rapidly biting, mutilating the inside of her mouth. Blood is spurting from her tongue.

The water is up to Jamey's chin now. Connie Lee's twisting head comes to a sudden stop. He hears the bones in her neck cracking. That beautiful smile has mutated into a maniacal grimace. Her eyes are gone...two black holes in their place. Though Jamey can see only the surface of the black eye sockets, he knows the holes are horrifically deep, ending in a place no one should ever see. Just behind the darkness he sees luminescent creatures found in the deepest part of the ocean. They dart furtively in and out of view. The preternaturally shimmering organisms are spelling out words. They are trying to convey primordial — abhorrent — secrets. They are trying to tell Jamey Maxwell the truth, but he is unable to comprehend.

And I ask, "Why does God have to do this to Jamey Maxwell?" The human I love most in this world. I know the answer.

Jamey Maxwell wakes up gasping for air. The telephone is ringing. He is not sure why he even bothered to have a telephone installed at his humble Dos Cruces abode. The one he calls St. Charles Place, in honor of his late father. Maybe he thought God would use the telephone instead of talking directly into his ear. God uses many methods of communication. Jamey picks up the phone.

"Hey you lazy son of a bitch, wake up. It's already 5:30 in the morning. Time to drop your cock and grab your socks." Thankfully it is not God. It is his old friend Jimmy Boyer, ex-U.S. Attorney, and now just an attorney.

"Jesus, Boyer, have you ever considered taking Valium?"

"No, but I wish I could get my hands on some fucking speed so I wouldn't have to sleep at all," Boyer replied. "You ready to get off your ass and go to work?"

"Haven't you heard, I retired five years ago?" Of course Jimmy Boyer knows this. They are good friends and have been for twenty years. Since Jamey was an up-and-coming customs agent and Jimmy was an up-and-coming assistant U.S. Attorney. Jimmy Boyer represented Jamey when he and Daniel, the goatboy, were arrested for the murder of Angelita Cavazos two years ago. Fortunately, all charges were dropped after the real murderers, *Los Diablos*, were found. Well, at least two of them, Dwayne Dubois and Luther Axelrod, were found. They were both pretty dead at the time though, thanks to Jamey and Marisol Cortinas, the late District Attorney of Losoya County. The third one, Jacinto Ocala, was never seen again. Ocala, aka "Chango," has become organic fertilizer for Jamey Maxwell's beloved brush country in South Texas. Chango is finally serving a useful purpose on this earth.

"I need your help," Jimmy says. Those are the magic words. Jamey could not, would not, refuse such a request from Jimmy Boyer.

"What's up?"

"A good friend of mine, a guy I went to high school and college with…his daughter and son-in-law were found murdered near Langtry last week. He is still in shock, but he wants someone to look into this as soon as possible. He doesn't trust the local fucking authorities to find who's responsible. Thought you might like to revisit your old stomping grounds. I hear West fucking Texas is fucking West Texas this time of year. Probably the first murder case they've had in those God-fucking-forsaken parts since Judge Roy Bean was around."

"What about the Texas Rangers?" Jamey asks.

"Oh, they're on the case too, but Scott doesn't trust those fuckers either. He thinks they'll keep things from him and Kay, won't tell them everything…and, of course, he's right. He wants somebody working for his team. So I suggested you, you lucky fucking bastard."

"Thanks for your vote of confidence. You know I'm not the man I used to be. Never was in fact. But at least I'm cheap. When and where do we meet?"

"How 'bout tomorrow at the Menger Hotel in San Antonio? Just to let you know, Bill and Kay are pretty well off…big in the S.A. local scene…I guess you could say heavy-hitters. Not sure if that means anything, but just thought it might be worth knowing. How 'bout 10 A.M.? Might be 'Miller Time'. Or are you on the fucking wagon, Maxwell?"

"The wheels fell off that wagon a long time ago. See you in the *mañana*."

Chapter 3

The Sit-down

I imagine you are wondering what it is like to be a Watcher. Well, this is one question where mankind's technology provides an easy answer. An analogy most of you can relate to: TIVO. Yes, the box you hook up to your television to record your sports, your soap operas, your game shows, and your so-called "reality TV." Most humans have no real concept of reality. Consider that a blessing. Jamey Maxwell is my TIVO. I can pause him in live action if I want. I can rewind him all the way back to his birth or anywhere between then and now. I can even do this with people he has encountered throughout his entire life if I want to, which I don't. Much too boring. But here's the really good part: I can fast forward him into the future. Up to a certain point. Towards the end, the tracking goes a little haywire. Horizontal and vertical holds cause the picture to become fuzzy, out of focus. It's just as well. I like surprises.

The Menger Hotel is an interesting place. It sits next to the Alamo. Both are historic, both sit in the middle of downtown San Antonio, and both appear much smaller than you would expect. How could you possibly fit so much history into these buildings? I will not, at this point, go into the potential correlation between the "last stand" at the Alamo and Jamey Maxwell's current and developing situation. Patience, my pretties…patience.

The Menger opened in 1859 and aimed to be "the finest hotel west of the Mississippi." Probably was. The hotel hosted both General Robert E. Lee and General Ulysses S. Grant. I doubt if there are many other hotels in Texas which can make that claim. Presidents McKinley, Taft, and Eisenhower all stayed here. Teddy Roosevelt recruited his Rough Riders at the Menger bar. Any bar good enough for Teddy and the Boys may be too good for Jamey Maxwell, at least in his opinion. Jamey's ego disappeared *hace muchos años*.

The Menger bar is a reproduction of the House of Lords' pub. Lots of wood and leather. Most people would feel important just sitting here. But in a moment, when Jamey Maxwell sits down next to his friend, Jimmy Boyer, and his client-to-be, Scott Stephenson, he will wish he was back in Dos Cruces. Boyer and Stephenson belong in a place like this, not Jamey Maxwell. This is a place for distinguished gentlemen, politicians, wheeler-dealers, high rollers. Jamey is none of these. He's just an ex-customs agent, apprentice *santero*, and shanghaied assassin of God. He knows this latter calling is why he is here. The other two at the table, the distinguished gentlemen, do not have a clue.

Jimmy Boyer and Scott Stephenson stand as soon as they see Jamey. Jimmy speaks first. "Scott, this is my old friend Jamey Maxwell."

Stephenson offers his hand, "Good to meet you, Jamey."

"I'm…I'm so sorry for your loss."

Stephenson grasps Jamey's hand harder and says, "I still can't believe it's real."

And looking at Stephenson through the eyes of an Old Testament prophet, Jamey replies, "You never will."

With that the three of them sit down.

Chapter 4

The Sorrow

Scott Stephenson begins to talk about his daughter, Kristin. At first he is talking to Jimmy Boyer and Jamey Maxwell, but after a few minutes he is talking to someone far away. Finally, looking down at the table, he speaks of a day some twenty years ago when he came home from work early. Kristin and her older sister, Casey, were playing in the backyard sandbox. Since it just happened to be close to a water faucet, the sandbox had become a mudbox. Scott recalls watching his daughters carrying their haute mud cuisine toward the house. "The look on Kristin's face was…I don't know…I guess you could call it solemn contentment. Like she knew to enjoy life now because of something she could see in the future. She was only two years old."

Jamey Maxwell understands where Scott Stephenson is coming from. Scott is struggling to hold on to a vision of his beloved daughter with which he can live. Even a bittersweet memory. Not the pictures, squirming in and out of his consciousness, of her dead body covered with dozens of scorpion-like creatures.

Scott cannot abide this. If these images are allowed to fester inside his brain, he will eventually kill himself. Yes, Jamey Maxwell, after the losses of so many close to him, understands all too well.

For Scott Stephenson, purging these pictures from his memory bank will be very difficult, particularly in the short term. The *San Antonio Light* has pounced upon this story like the proverbial duck on a junebug. Or more like a sleazy reporter on a tragic story. After interviewing witnesses, including the guileless sheep-herder, Manuelito Castillo, and gathering all the gory details, the press has dubbed this headline case "The Vinegaroon Murders." And since most people don't have a clue what a vinegaroon is, but realize the word, when combined with the word 'murder', has a most intriguing ring to it, they are buying the newspaper in record numbers. No, it will not be easy for Scott Stephenson to banish the horrible images of his deceased daughter from his brain.

Jamey gently tries to bring Scott back to the present. They must talk about the murders of Scott's daughter and son-in-law. To begin the investigation, Jamey needs background information. Potential suspects. Potential witnesses. He wants to mitigate the pain the questions will cause, but knows that will be impossi-ble.

Pain. To us angels, the most amazing thing about human beings is your capacity for pain. God created pain, but He cannot feel pain. He believes that He feels pain, but He doesn't. It just makes Him excited, agitat-ed. And neither do most angels know pain, especially those up the celestial ladder. The closer to God, the less capacity for agony. Powers, Virtues, Principalities tend to go dormant when they witness suffering of any kind. Thrones and Dominions ignore pain. Cherubim are never exposed to pain, thanks be to God, for they would shatter like fine crystal. Seraphs, or Watchers, like me, are closer to man, so every once in a while we experience a brief sensation approximating pain, but it's just a glimpse. Guardian angels, what Watchers like to call pseudo-angels, however, can feel pain quite acutely. But only physical pain.

I've been around since the beginning of time, *todo el tiempo,* as we would say here in Del Rio, so I've observed mankind's endurance for pain and suffering. I stand in awe of this...and I weep.

I was there in Jerusalem during the Crusades. I saw the catapults, the boiling oil, the crossbows, the swords...all wielded in the name of God. I was there in Madrid during the Spanish Inquisition. I saw the dungeons, the racks, the iron maidens, the interrogations...all sanctioned in the name of God. I was there at Krakow in 1943. I saw children rent from their mothers. Mothers who knew they would never see those children again. Many of those mothers survived. Most of them chose to live. Most of them chose not to hate God, even though He could have saved their children, had He chosen to. That's why I know God is unable to feel pain. So when I speak of my wonder of human endurance for pain, I speak of physical pain, of mental pain, and most of all, of spiritual pain. And, I speak of the cruel irony of God's apparent apathy in these matters.

Jamey says, "Scott, I need to ask some tough questions. I want to help you find out who killed Kristin and Billy. Are you up for this?"

"Yes. I know revenge will not bring my wife and me peace. But neither will no revenge. I'm not even going to call it justice because that's not how it feels. And I'm worried about Casey. Whoever killed Kristin may come after her. Or my wife, Kay. I'm not worried about myself. Not only do I not fear death now, I would..." Scott doesn't bother to finish the sentence. He knows Jamey understands.

"So you think it may be someone who has a grudge against your entire family?" Jamey asks.

"I don't know. As an attorney, I deal with all types of people, including mean and crazy ones. But in the last few years I've been pretty much dealing exclusively in real estate law and it's an area hard for anyone to get that worked up over. To the point of murder? I don't think so, but who knows? And why not come after me...why Kristin and Billy?"

Jamey replies, "I've learned never to underestimate the human potential for evil. At this point, we don't want to rule anyone either in or out. And Scott, that includes you and your wife, and even Casey. I don't want to sound too blunt, but I don't know how else to say it. In most murder cases the perpetrator is a relative. So let's take a few minutes to rule out family members."

Jamey already knew that the murders were not committed by a family member. God had intimated as much. But Jamey didn't think now, or ever for that matter, was a good time to tell Scott Stephenson and Jimmy Boyer about his special relationship with the

Man Upstairs. So for the next half hour Jamey goes through the motion of listening to the various alibis for the family members, including aunts, uncles, nieces, nephews, etc. Then Jamey says, "Let's move on to friends and acquaintances. Did Kristin work? Did she have any enemies that you know of? Start with friends."

Scott smiled, "She had lots of friends. People were drawn to Kristin. She was beautiful, inside and out. She was nice to everyone, especially those she felt were broken in some way. She loved underdogs. But really close friends? Only two or three. Let's see...Molly and Lacey Hunter...they're sisters... friends since elementary school. They're both married now and live in Houston and Galveston. Vanessa Scofield, a friend from high school. She's married to Brad Scofield...the automobile Scofields. They live here, in San Antonio. Kristin has never worked, so no coworkers. And as far as enemies, like I said, everyone loved Kristin." Scott pauses, the thought of someone not loving Kristin inconceivable to him.

"Kay and I believe this was a kidnap. A kidnap gone bad. Maybe someone did it for money and then lost their nerve. Of course they couldn't let Kristin and Billy go if that happened. Kay and I are not wealthy by today's standards, but others may not know that. And besides, people will do amazingly bad things for very little money." Scott Stephenson, tears forming, does not want to quit talking about his dead daughter. But he does.

Jamey is quiet for a moment, already knowing where he will start looking. Just a gut feeling...God's gut. But he is not ready to share with the rest of the class. So he says, "Scott, I would like you and Kay to sit down and make a list of your clients over the last five years. Also, a list of people that you have ever made angry…even if it didn't seem like much at the time. And a list of people that you know, at any level, personal, professional, who might have financial problems. Get Casey to do the same thing." Jamey is hoping this will give Scott, his wife, and his daughter, a temporary outlet for their grief.

Scott Stephenson, Jimmy Boyer and Jamey Maxwell speak another few minutes about nothing, waiting for a good place to stop. They find it when Jamey says, "Well, with my short attention span, I need to get back to my hotel and make a few notes…make a couple of calls. I'll get started on this and keep you both posted."

Jimmy Boyer replies, "No need to keep me in the loop unless there's something you need. Other than that, just keep this between the two of you. I think it's better that way."

With that, the three of them say their rather awkward goodbyes and leave the venerable Menger Hotel. Jamey walks to his old truck with visions of his own two daughters, no longer of this earth, in his increasingly unstable mind. But the funny thing is, the more unstable his mind grows the more focused he becomes. God's plan, I suppose.

Before I move on, I want to share an observation about Jimmy Boyer. I am hesitant to do this, because I fear it will make me look somewhat superficial. And, God knows, Seraphs are not supposed to be superficial. But here it is: Jimmy Boyer is married to a big, fat woman. A human male, tall, handsome, intelligent, charming, who causes virtually every human female to swoon in his presence. Yet, he chose to marry a "full-figured" woman who has since expanded to at least two hundred and fifty pounds, displacing limited space on a limited planet. And she is not seven feet tall. Maybe five foot two…and, yes, her eyes are blue. He is madly in love with her. Did I just say madly? True love in humans is beyond bizarre. Any arguments out there in the Peanut Gallery? I didn't think so. I will speak more of Jimmy Boyer and his wife, Loretta, as we spend more time together.

Anyway, here's my deal. As do most Seraphs, I value beauty, physical beauty, maybe just a little too much. As a Watcher, I find Jimmy Boyer's wife very difficult to watch. And his love for her is even more difficult to watch. Maybe I *am* superficial. *No le hace.*

Jamey Maxwell is back in his bed at St. Charles Place, asleep. In the dream, Jimmy Boyer is talking to him. "Hey, you cocksucker, you up for this? It's gonna be harder than my dick in Angelita's ass with Loretta watching. Get my fucking drift? I'm afraid you're just a big pussy now that your bitchy wife and your pathetic ugly daughters are dead."

Jamey's eyes spring open, instantly forgetting this little nightmare. He wants to kill someone.

Chapter 5

The Scum

I will tell you who committed the murders of Kristin and Billy Garnett, but you must promise not to tell Jamey Maxwell. God has ordained that Jamey must perform due diligence in his search for the killers (with just an occasional hint from me). I trust you to keep a secret. It's something you humans are so good at. So here it is: the murderers are Vanessa and Bradley Scofield. Yes, of those Scofields.

Scofield Chevrolet, Scofield Honda, Scofield Cadillac, Scofield Autoplex, Scofield Auto Megamart, Scofield Gently-Owned Auto Store, etc. There is *beaucoup* money in selling cars. Just look at a couple of other San Antonio car dealers: Red McCombs, ex-owner of the Minnesota Vikings; Tom Benson, owner of the New Orleans Saints. The Scofield family has chosen to invest its fortune in what they consider a far more enjoyable and worthy venture…themselves.

Bradley Scofield is third generation rich. The generation where things start to fall apart. Covetousness, conceit, and the conviction that God means for them to have copious quantities of cash, culminate to commence the collapse. Bradley Scofield is the poster child for visible sanctity.

Vanessa Scofield was not a natural born Scofield, but she got into the swing of things, e. g. spending lots of money, quite naturally, and quite quickly, upon marrying Bradley. Kind of like the bumper sticker that says: "I Wasn't Born In Texas But I Got Here As Soon As I Could." Bradley was the prototypical spoiled little rich kid. And Vanessa became one. They have more money than brains. They have more money than conscience. They have more than enough money to become heartless, soulless murderers.

The ever-amazing naive narcissists: human beings. God and angels love you. Yes, we do. Most of you, anyway. We also hate many of you. To paraphrase your singer/songwriter, Carly Simon: "You're so vain, you probably think this world is about you." Think about it. You think God created an entire, virtually empty, universe just for you. Even though you will never experience more than an immeasurably tiny iota of it. At most, a small blue remote planet; the bleak, gray dust-covered remote moon orbiting this remote planet; with a whole lot of luck, a bleak, red dust-covered remote planet next door; all contained in an isolated, nondescript remote solar system on the outer fringes of the universe. Does this make any sense at all? Why would God go to that much trouble? For your amusement? To give you something to ponder for the brief flicker of your individually insignificant lives? Many of you doubt there are any other life forms in the entire fucking universe. Do you ever think there may be a secret here beyond your understanding? I hope that possibility has crossed your collective mind. Otherwise you will fall into the category of humans that we Watchers love to hate.

And then you have the gall to ask Him to choose whatever country you live in over every other country on earth. Or whatever state you live in over all other states in your country. Or whatever sports team you root for over all other sports teams. Or Boy Scout troop, Masonic Lodge, VFW post, ballet class, etceteras. "Dear God, please help us kick the shit out of the low-life Longhorns." You sometimes even have the nerve to demand his approval. Your song "God Bless America" sounds like an order, not a request. Next time you sing it, you might want to consider squeezing the word "please" in between "God" and "Bless." Remember my earlier admonition about the one and only mortal sin in God's eyes: presumptuousness. Just a little reminder.

Vanessa Scofield is a living testament to the power of money. She is at least 75 pounds overweight, according to her society's standard. Fifty pounds overweight compared to the ordinary, run-of-the-mill, boring, virtually imperceptible society in whence most of you other humans live; and from whence Vanessa Scofield was issued. Vanessa has a plethora of prior and present unpleasant qualities, not the least being her personality. But money has resolved most of those nuisances. Neiman Marcus: Let me hear an "Amen!" Saks Fifth Avenue: Let me hear a "Hallelujah!" Plastic surgery: Let me hear "Praise the Lord!" It's amazing how so-called filthy lucre can transform you from corpulent and petulant bitch to Rubenesque princess.

Remind me to tell you how Vanessa managed to

acquire Bradley Scofield. It involved embellishments, garnishes, plus an amazing variety of sex acts.

Oh yes, the motive for the murders of Billy and Kristin Garnett? How shall I put this delicately? Well, let us just say that Bradley Scofield was attracted to Kristin Garnett. He thought she was beautiful. She was. And I'm not talking about Neiman Marcus/Saks Fifth Avenue beauty. I'm talking about a natural beauty which is a rare and precious commodity. Kristin was physically beautiful. She looked like a young Grace Kelly. But Kristin, more importantly, or should I say more unfortunately, possessed an even rarer beauty: beauty of the soul. It got her killed along with her young husband, Billy. His crime was being married to Kristin.

To be less delicate, however, one night when Brad Scofield was both drunk and high on Ecstasy he said these magic words to his wife, Vanessa: "Man, I would love to fuck Kristin." Those seven words became Kristin Garnett's death warrant.

Chapter 6

The Scene

Bradley and Vanessa Scofield are "in with the in-crowd." They are the in-crowd. In the local society news, in the Fiesta events, in the debutante balls, in the courtside seats at Spurs games, in the New Year's Eve bashes, in the nightclubs *du jour*, even in the underground raves...they are omnipresent. Vanessa is naturally ostentatious. A slightly more feminine version of your famous lesbian ex-talk show host, Rosie O'Donnell. Brad is exceptionally unostentatious, but with the trappings of money. He looks like a mannequin one would find at a fine men's clothing store, complete with the wardrobe, but with less of a personality. And with less of a soul.

Free will, shall we discuss? Many humans (and some angels) believe in free will. They believe God created us and then said, "Go forth and amuse Me." But like most things involving God, which is everything, it's not that simple. Here's an analogy that you might relate to: when you're driving a car and take your hands off the wheel, at that moment, the car has free will. Then there are degrees of free will. If you're driving a car and you're drunk, then you're not totally in control but the car does not have total free will. Earth is a giant freeway and God is behind the wheels of six billion automobiles. Sometimes He is in control; sometimes His mind wanders; sometimes He is intoxicated or otherwise impaired; sometimes He gets out of a car entirely. And sometimes He's mad as hell and He's not going to take it anymore. Now imagine God overcome by road rage and Jamey Maxwell as the vehicle. The opposite end of the free will spectrum. Kind of scary.

Vanessa Kaplan was Kristin Stephenson's friend in high school. Or at least Kristin thought Vanessa was her friend. But what Vanessa wanted from Kristin was the "connection." The connection to a pretty girl. The connection to a popular girl. The connection to a girl that Vanessa thought was rich. This trifecta was going to get Vanessa to the next level. The level where an unattractive, unpopular, unrich girl gets to marry an attractive, popular, rich guy. It worked. The fact that Bradley Scofield was also an arrogant asshole was actually an additional turn-on for Vanessa Kaplan.

Vanessa was a parasite. No, that's wrong. Parasites almost always provide some form of reciprocity to their host in return for their existence. Instead, Vanessa was a bloodsucker. A vampire. She sucked the marrow from Kristin's soul. And why did Kristin allow this? There are many mysteries embedded within the human race and this is one of them. Kristin felt sorry for Vanessa. Because of Vanessa's previously mentioned shortcomings, Kristin wanted to help her. But that doesn't really explain it. Maybe it was Kristin's naiveté. Maybe it was because Vanessa was the consummate actress, evoking sympathy at will. Maybe it was because Kristin had a soul too beautiful for this world. Or maybe it was part of God's warped plan. Whatever the reason, during her senior year Vanessa finally hit pay dirt when Kristin introduced her to Bradley Scofield IV. The result: a regrettable merger.

Once Vanessa set her sights on Bradley Scofield, the hunt was almost over. As your Mary Poppins would say, "Well begun is half done." She had him bagged, gutted, and mounted before he knew what hit him. Such a trophy. Within two months after meeting him, Vanessa lost forty pounds. She accomplished this by not eating; by making herself vomit when, out of necessity, she had to eat; by taking diuretics and laxatives several times a day; and by actually exercising for the first time in her life. This unique effort in self-improvement lasted just two months. By then she was only twenty or thirty pounds overweight. She compensated by disguising herself in very trendy clothes, very trendy makeup, very trendy accessories, and revealing a very sophisticated grasp of what sex, and the promise of sex, does to a young human male. With this smoke and mirror-on-the-ceiling approach, she obtained Brad Scofield. He never had a chance.

Brad Scofield's parents were, needless to say, not enamored of his relationship with Vanessa Kaplan. But they thought it was harmless; just a phase. Month by month their concern grew, however, as they could see that Brad was actually getting serious about this…this hussy. That's how they saw her. Her disguise was not effective with them. They saw her as a gold digger and they were right as rain. They tried telling Brad countless times, and each time his desire for Vanessa increased incrementally, until it reached the point at which he had to possess her. He liked possessing things and he did not like being told "no." What he did not understand is that he was the possessee, not the possessor. Not that it made much difference in the scheme of things. They were together. That's all that mattered. After not letting him out of her sight for three years, Vanessa hit the love lottery. Bradley Scofield proposed.

Despite the futile objections of his parents, Brad married Vanessa in a huge Who's Who wedding event on Brad's twenty-first birthday. It just so happens, that is the day Bradley William Herbert Scofield IV inherited his $10,000,000 trust fund. That night, on their honeymoon, Vanessa Scofield had the first, and only, orgasm of her life. And, trust me when I tell you this: it was the trust fund that did it.

Greed. It is the antithesis to your human capacity for pain. Your desire to acquire money, power, things…stuff. You humans like your stuff. Many think this is purely a product of western civilization, particularly capitalism. But let me assure you, it is not. Greed crosses cultural, racial, religious, sexual boundaries. It is the quintessential human trait. As if God inserted a greed gene when creating you. You see a young black man in America, say a senior in high school, eighteen years old, with a rare and coveted talent, the ability to play a children's game: the game of basketball. Then you see adults around him scrambling to take advantage of this talent by unduly influencing him, not for his sake, but for the sake of greed. This young man of poverty has survived these eighteen years not through worldly possessions, but through the love of family and friends. But that all dissipates, evaporates. The lifelong connections of love and friendship are no longer important. What is important is that they all want to get rich off this young man so they can all acquire. Acquire fancy SUVs, acquire diamond jewelry, acquire $1,000 sneakers…acquire stuff…*bling bling* in the current vernacular. It should be quite disconcerting to you humans just how tenuous love is in the face of greed.

Now there are some notable exceptions: in modern times, Florence Nightingale, Mahatma Ghandi, Oskar Schindler, and others, including a man many on Earth believe is the second or third coming of Satan himself, Osama bin Laden. Let's ponder this for a moment. Here is a man born a millionaire in Saudi Arabia with all of the luxuries in the world at his beck and call. Yet, he gave it all up to become a freedom fighter in Afghanistan against the Soviet occupation. Later to be judged the most infamous terrorist in history; his sworn enemy, the entire western world. Everyone on Earth knows the story so I will not go into it. But I ask you this: how is it that in the world of humans, greed can conquer love while hate can conquer greed?

I know you are dying to hear how Kristin and Billy died, aren't you? You want the gory details, right? Well, for your salacious edification, here goes. As I have told you, Kristin Garnett's death sentence was decreed shortly after Brad Scofield said these words to his wife: "Man, I would love to fuck Kristin." Billy Garnett, a classic case of guilt by association. Vanessa was judge, jury, and more than willing executioner. Brad's participation was not optional.

Death. As I look out the window of my sad trailer, across from the trailer park I see four cows grazing amongst the sparse desert grass. I see death…the four cows are dying. I decide to escape my depressing abode to hover above the trailer park. I see one of my neighbors, an elderly widow, tending a wilted geranium in one of her many outdoor pots. I see death…both the old woman and the plant are dying. I rise further on the thermals and can now see the entire city of Del Rio. I see hundreds, perhaps thousands, of people…in their cars, walking the streets, in their backyards. I see death. Each and every one of them is dying. I continue to ride the upward flow of life-giving air, heated by greenhouse gases, toxic byproducts of human existence and nature, or God, if you will. I can now see most of West Texas, from Uvalde to Alpine. I can see a surprising amount of green vegetation…mesquite trees, juniper, creosote, a multitude of cacti, grasses…surprising in that this is a desert. I see death…all of this plant life, and the animal life it supports, is dying. I can almost smell the stench. If I chose to ride higher, into the stratosphere and beyond (and I could do that), I would be able to see this entire, beautiful blue-green planet covered with so much sustenance…water, fertile soil, precious greenery, the vast rain forests and grasslands, but, in the end, all I would really see is death. Death on a microscopic scale; death on a trivial scale; death on a middling scale; death on a grand scale; death on a universal scale…for all of you are dying. Your forests are dying; your oceans are dying; your cities are dying; your planet is dying; your solar system is dying; your galaxy is dying; your universe is dying…could it be your God is dying as well?

You ask what was the real motive behind the murders? To this I respond with questions for you: What is a human being? What was a Ted Bundy? What was a Jeffrey Dahmer? What was a Luther Axelrod? What is an Andrea Yates? What is a Susan Smith? What are Brad and Vanessa Scofield? And here is the answer to your question about the murders of Billy and Kristin Garnett, in the form of an algebraic equation:

$$2M = \frac{\text{insanity}^2 + \text{zeal} \times \text{jealousy} \pm \text{competence}}{\text{opportunity}}$$

The challenging part for Vanessa was deciding when, where, and how. The why was obvious as far as she was concerned. When Brad Scofield sobered up and came down from his Ecstasy high, he was informed that Kristin must exit this world. Brad, being the partially brain-dead, fully pussy-whipped (in impolite human parlance) husband, didn't offer much resistance. Besides, it sounded kind of exciting to him. He was hoping maybe, just maybe, Vanessa would let him perform a few creative sexual experiments upon Kristin, prior to the final act. He thought he might broach this subject, diplomatically, when Vanessa was in one of her rare good moods.

If you imagined that Vanessa would give the slightest pause to murdering her ostensible best friend, then you would be exceedingly wrong. She approached the task with glee. She planned with enthusiasm, reveling in all of the possibilities. She was in hog heaven and she was the porcine deity. She was large-and-in-charge. Vanessa shared most of her ideas with Brad, always probing for breaches in his conscience. Not a problem. Bradley Scofield has no conscience. Had Brad expressed any second thoughts or reservations, Vanessa would simply have added him to her hit list. For the first time in her life, she felt the power. It was an aphrodisiac. Her sex drive hit overdrive and Brad was forced to perform at will. And, although she never repeated the monetarily-induced orgasm of her wedding night, she relished the feeling of control over her husband and her world.

Vanessa finally arrived at a definitive plan. It proved to be a good one. It seems she had an affinity for this line of work. She would invite Billy and Kristin to the Scofield Ranch near Kerrville for a weekend of good times with good friends. Billy and Kristin had visited the ranch several years earlier and hated every minute of it. But they hid their discontentment quite admirably. Billy didn't care for either Brad or Vanessa and neither did Kristin, but she was never able to admit it. Even to herself. Well, she did tell Billy that Brad gave her the "willies," but she tried to be a true friend to Vanessa. Billy was never able to understand, but he loved Kristin and figured there must be some redeeming social value to Vanessa Scofield. He was, of course, wrong. And then they died.

Here is how it all went down. First, the faux plan. At 8:00 P.M. Friday night, May 12, Brad and Vanessa were to meet Billy and Kristin in the parking lot of Kroger supermarket near downtown Kerrville. From there, Billy and Kristin would follow their hosts out of

Kerrville along the winding state highway toward Medina for five miles, taking a right on County Road 6610 for another three miles, through the locked gate to the Scofield Ranch, and then another mile to the cedar and limestone lodge. This was the scenario, the charade, Vanessa had conjured for her guests.

What actually happened was this: at 7:30 P.M., Bradley Scofield walked to the horse barn about one hundred yards from the lodge on Scofield Ranch. There he got into the 1998 Jeep Cherokee used by the hired hands (and covered with their fingerprints) for hauling feed and pulling one of several small horse trailers, and headed to Kerrville to meet the Garnetts. At the same time, Vanessa called Dora Ambriz, the live-in maid/cook, and asked her to come upstairs to the bedroom suite. It so happened, Dora had just sat down to watch her second favorite Mexican novella, *El Mundo Peligroso*. This was not a coincidence. Vanessa knew of Dora's fondness for this particular soap opera and had molded her strategy around it. Within thirty seconds, Dora, with dutifully disguised disgust, knocked on Vanessa's door. From inside the suite, Dora could hear Brad Scofield's raised voice, apparently from the suite's bathroom, asking Vanessa to bring him a towel. Vanessa yelled back, "Just a minute," and opened the door. There Dora, wearing the sweetest smile and harboring the most unkind feelings towards Vanessa, Brad, and the entire Scofield clan, said, "Yes, ma'am?"

"Dora, Brad and I are soooo hungry. Would you mind fixing us some *quesadillas*? And some of your wonderful *guacamole*? Bring us a couple of Heinekens, too. Just a snack until our guests arrive. We don't want to get too stuffed. Thanks."

"Yes, ma'am." Dora wished she knew more about poisons and such.

Within fifteen minutes, Dora, ever so efficient, was back knocking at Brad and Vanessa's door. This time she heard Brad's voice yelling, "Vanessa, can you get that? I'm in my underwear." The thought of seeing Brad Scofield in his underwear sent the most uncomfortable shivers up, sideways, and down Dora Ambriz' spine. She was relieved when Vanessa answered the door and Brad was nowhere in sight. She carried the tray filled with the requested snacks into the bedroom and set it on the small round table in the corner. Dora's tunnel vision couldn't have been any more tunneled. The specter of a virtually naked Brad Scofield made her nauseous. She hastened from the second floor suite back to her sparsely furnished room hoping to see a virtually naked Enrique Peña on her TV set. He was her idol, her fantasy; and this time she was counting on him to wipe *la visión repugnante* of Brad Scofield from her brain. A daunting task, indeed.

At 8:00 P.M., the phone in Dora's room rang again. Again, it was Vanessa. "Dora, any sign of our guests yet?"

"No ma'am," replied Dora. "Not yet."

"Well, I hope they didn't get lost. They've only been here once before and that was a few years ago. They'll get here soon, I'm sure. In the meantime, could you bring us a couple more Heinekens?"

"Yes ma'am," you *pinche gringa* bitch, thought Dora.

Within a few minutes, Dora was back at the *pinche gringa's* door. This time when she knocked, she heard

Brad Scofield shout, "Get the fuckin' door, will ya?" He sounded drunk, which was not to the slightest degree unusual in Dora's experience. Brad was almost always drunk when visiting the ranch. This time Vanessa opened the door and took the tray with the two beers from Dora and rolled her eyes, as if to say, "Men, can't live with 'em and they make lousy sausage."

At 8:30 P.M., Vanessa rang Dora's room at the exact moment the highlight of her week was to begin. The opening credits of her very most favorite soap opera, *El Amor Es Un Infierno*, were just beginning to roll. "Dora, be a dear and bring us a couple of beers," Vanessa giggled at her near rhyme. Dora was not amused. She scurried upstairs, knocked on the door and heard Brad yelling, "That son of a bitch!" She handed the tray to Vanessa and scurried downstairs, hoping she had not missed anything important. She was in love with the lead actor, Javier Solís. He was *muy guapo.*

As soon as she knew Dora was back in her room watching her favorite TV show, Vanessa headed for the horse barn. She walked swiftly for a fat girl. When she opened the barn door she found things to be in order. Her plan was going well. Billy and Kristin Garnett were on their knees, hands bound behind their backs with the ever so versatile duct tape, duct tape across their mouths, and a Browning .12 gauge pointed at their heads. The Jeep Cherokee was in the barn, along with Billy and Kristin Garnett's Lincoln Navigator.

Billy and Kristin had thought it was strange when Brad pulled his vehicle into the horse barn and then waved them in, but they never imagined it was anything other than an eccentric millionaire thing. Brad waved them around the Jeep and they pulled in front and parked the car. When Billy Garnett stepped out of the Lincoln, Brad was holding the shotgun on him. He told Kristin to get out of the car and come around to the driver's side or he would blow Billy's head off. Brad told Billy to put his hands behind his back. He handed Kristin the roll of duct tape and told her to wrap it around Billy's hands. Then he told her to place a piece of tape over Billy's mouth. When Billy was secured, Brad took the duct tape and repeated the process with Kristin. Bradley Scofield had successfully completed his assignment. A rare occurrence indeed. But his lovely wife Vanessa had made it very clear that he best not fuck up. Much to his disappointment, Brad never got the courage to ask Vanessa if he could try a couple of new "things" on Kristin. By this time, Brad had figured out what a dangerous woman he had married and discretion being the better part of valor, decided not to broach the subject of having any kind of sex with Kristin Garnett. He had seen what just one mention of it had wrought. He didn't want to wind up on the wrong team. What Brad had not figured out is this: if he had fucked up this part of the plan, he was on his own. Vanessa would just say, "I can't believe my husband would do such a thing." Plausible denial is a wonderful concept.

Vanessa's plan did not allow any extra time for banter or taunting, much to her chagrin. She would have so liked to have told Kristin how much she had always hated her. How she always looked down on her. How she thought Kristin was a fake, a fraud, a bitch. Instead, she simply said, "Brad, shoot Billy." Brad looked at his very significant other, realized this was a direct order not to be disobeyed, looked back down at Billy Garnett, and pulled the trigger. I won't go into the result, other than to say it was effective.

"Hand me the gun," Vanessa said and Brad did. By now, Kristin Garnett knew it was over and was quietly sobbing. Even at the end, under the most horrendous circumstances which a human being could be placed, she exuded grace, beauty, and courage. Then, the second shot. Phase I was complete.

Vanessa was neither elated nor upset. She had a job to do and she was going to do it well. As I said earlier, Vanessa had a knack for this kind of work. Now deeply into her efficient mode, she ordered Brad to start cleaning up. They had been rehearsing for several weeks and even a slacker like Bradley Scofield knew what to do. With an assortment of shovels, rakes, plastic bags, gloves, etc., Brad started the process of eliminating evidence. He was surprised to find he was not the least bit squeamish. This, needless to say, had been the most excitement he had experienced in his entire, uneventful until now, affluent life. Brad is the type to get bored easily. So instead of being squeamish, he was already coming down from his short-lived high wondering how he was ever going to top this in his lifetime. The fact that he was having to gather and dispose of human blood and tissue did not bother him, except for the fact that he had always hated having to clean up after himself. It didn't seem fair. *Pobrecito.*

Vanessa discarded her comfortable full-length dress, under which she was naked, and her flip flops, handing them to Brad. She changed into an identical dress and flip flops which she had secreted in the tack room and returned to the lodge. For the next two hours, Vanessa called Dora repeatedly, each time sounding more concerned about her tardy guests and each time requesting more beer. And each time Dora knocked on the door to her employer's suite, she would hear Brad Scofield's voice, sounding a little drunker and a little creepier. The last call came at 10:30 P.M., just when her Spanish language news program was going off the air.

Brad had spent the last four hours or so cleaning up the crime scene. He wrapped the bodies in plastic sheeting, loaded them into the back of the Jeep, and covered them with empty brown paper feed bags. Brad meticulously wiped down the shotgun, removing all prints, then sprayed it with WD-40. The Browning .12 gauge was placed under the backseat of the Jeep which the Mexican workers used daily. Brad then cleaned himself in the small bathroom in the barn. He stripped to his underwear (a phantom image still burned into Dora's retinas) washed repeatedly, and changed into clean clothes. Brad had taken his and Vanessa's murder clothes, along with a plastic bag filled with blood and tissue-soaked hay and dirt, and placed them in an empty fifty-five gallon drum used for burning trash. The trash barrel was located on the opposite side of the barn from the house, about 100 feet away. As per Vanessa's instructions, he waited until 1:00 A.M. to start the fire. At 1:45 A.M., when he was sure the evidence had burned as much as possible, Brad used a garden hose to extinguish any remaining embers. He thoroughly washed the burn can and a twenty foot radius around it. He scooped the remaining ashes into four plastic bags. Brad then placed the four bags of evidence in the back of the Jeep. Vanessa would later add the burned remains of the cassette tape with Brad's voice on it, created exclusively for Dora Ambriz' benefit, to one of the plastic bags.

The rest of the plan involved waiting until 2:00 A.M. and driving Billy and Kristin's vehicle back to the Kroger parking lot. Vanessa, wearing gloves, drove the Lincoln and Brad followed in the Jeep. They left the Lincoln in the exact spot where Brad had found Billy and Kristin parked earlier. Before leaving the ranch, Vanessa cautioned Brad to drive slowly, but not too slowly, and she did the same. Once the Lincoln was parked, Vanessa carefully surveyed the scene around the Kroger parking lot. Seeing no signs of police officers, security guards, drunken teenagers out past curfew, or any other inconvenient eyewitnesses, she got into the Jeep with her ever more obedient husband. Now the challenging part: they had to drive to an area in West Texas near Seminole Canyon State Park, dispose of the bodies and return to the Scofield Ranch in less than five hours. They would deposit one bag of burned evidence in receptacles at each of the four roadside parks along the route.

Before the murders, Vanessa and Brad had spent several days scouting areas near Langtry and found a ranch accessible by a remote county-maintained road. And, not coincidentally, Vanessa, who had done her homework, knew this was a county road traversed daily by the United States Border Patrol. She had watched as the Border Patrol officers, at day's end, dragged behind their vehicle an eight-foot wooden rake for a two-mile stretch over this road. This allows the Border Patrol to detect new footprints of those "pesky" illegal immigrants who migrate across this ranch on a daily basis in search of a life. How ironic. Vanessa was quite sure it would take at least two or three days to find the bodies and by then, the Border Patrol would have erased any tire prints that could be used as evidence in a court of law. And, worst case scenario, if the vehicle was traced back to them, there were various Hispanic employees, of both legal and illegal variety, who worked on the Scofield Ranch. These folks would undoubtedly be blamed for the murders. Unfortunately, their fingerprints would be all over the vehicle. And since Vanessa and Brad wore gloves the entire time they were disposing of the evidence, the Scofields' fingerprints would not be found. Anyway, what motivation would the Scofields have for murdering their best friends? It had to be those "damned greedy Meskins." Vanessa was proud of her new found talent for plotting murders. She discovered that it was almost as much fun as shopping at the Galleria in Houston.

As Vanessa drove toward the Galvan Ranch, she had to stifle a giggle after a brain flash. Maybe she could organize a new community education class entitled Murder 101. The first class could be "How to Dispose of Bodies."

Originally, Vanessa's plan called for her husband to dispose of the bodies by himself. But for good reason she did not trust him to do it right. She was afraid he would get tired of driving, or just sober up and decide he didn't like traveling in the same vehicle as dead people and drop them off at a roadside park. She wasn't going to take any unnecessary chances. However, this created the most difficult problem of the whole scenario. To make this trip in five hours without speeding was cutting it close. She had Brad fill four 5 gallon gasoline containers so they would not have to stop at any public places along the way. And they had to be back at Scofield Ranch, and in their room, by 7:00 A.M. That's when Dora promptly served Vanessa and Brad's favorite breakfast, *huevos rancheros.*

Vanessa's immaculate planning was complemented by several fortuitous twists. First, Billy and Kristen, although close to their respective families, had, as a couple, an independent streak. They seldom told anyone about their plans. No one knew they had planned to visit the Scofield Ranch on their final weekend on Earth. Brad and Vanessa Scofield, for obvious reasons, had told no one, except Dora Ambriz, that the Garnetts were coming to visit. It was not until the following Monday, when Billy failed to show up at work, that anyone missed them. It took another two days for Billy's employer to track down family members. Another two days were needed to complete the procedure to report missing persons. Another day passed before an All Points Bulletin was issued. Next, because of the nature of the wounds, the amount of time the bodies had been allowed to decompose before discovery, and because there were no fingerprint records of the Garnetts, identification took almost two weeks. Finally, almost three weeks passed before the Assistant Manager of the Kroger store in Kerrville reported an abandoned Lincoln Navigator in the parking lot. By the time all of this information was put together, this new case was already a "cold case." All of the law enforcement officials involved, with the exception of Torres County Deputy Luis Moya, convinced each other that this was a robbery or carjacking gone awry. Moya believed the *alacranes del diablo* held the key to solving the murders. However, after a lifetime of being dismissed as a defective human, Luis decided to keep this to himself. For now.

There is no such thing as evil. It is a concept without merit. The closest thing to evil on Earth is insanity enhanced by poor decision-making. The number one purported evildoer on your planet, Adolph Hitler, was just a crazy guy doing crazy things. One thing led to another, Poland led to France, etc., until it got thoroughly out of hand. Even Satan-el, or the devil to you humans, has been unfairly vilified, taken out of context, misunderstood. He loves God. God loves him. They just can't get along. So one should be careful when judging others, or as the Bible says, "judge not, lest ye be judged." Being mistaken for evil can happen to anyone, especially humans, since all of you are insane to one degree or another.

Chapter 7

The Society

Jamey Maxwell feels like a fish out of *agua*. He hates parties. Especially pretentious parties full of pretentious people. And this one has exceeded the government daily maximum pretentiousness limits. The only thing missing is Martha Stewart as the hostess. But it is clear this hostess is a Stewart devotee. And if Martha, aka M. Diddy, decided to move to French Guyana and start a commune, as did the Reverend Jim Jones; and then Martha decided to serve watercress sandwiches and chamomile tea spiked with cyanide; this hostess would be the first to demurely ask for the recipe; then, of course, for seconds. "It's a good thing."

Jimmy Boyer and Scott Stephenson invited Jamey because they thought he might be able to find some leads in his exceedingly preliminary murder investigation. This is the crowd the victims grew up with.

Jamey Maxwell has managed to pull together an ensemble — a costume he would call it — comprised of his only jacket, brown wool with elbow patches; tan slacks he borrowed from brother Robert years ago; an old blue dress shirt; and an old blue tie. He did finally break down and buy underwear. Something old, something new, something borrowed, something blue. He wore his old boots too. He washed them with a dirty dish rag and smeared some brown shoe polish on them. As his old customs agent partner, Big Al, would say: "Looks like you polished them with a Hershey Bar."

But so far all Jamey has found is a comfortable overstuffed sofa in a quiet corner of the luxury town home with a beautiful night view of the San Antonio downtown skyline. He is sadly aware of the incongruity of having a party such as this so soon after the murders of two young people who should have been guests here tonight. Although made up of humans, high society, Jamey realizes, is a self-perpetuating apparatus devoid of conscience. It must maintain itself at all costs. Party plans had been made and they must be sustained. He wishes he was not here. Jamey's mind is drifting into dangerously depressing terrain when he is not-so-rudely interrupted. He doesn't consider it rude because he wanted to be rescued from *muy malas* memories and because the interruptor happens to be a very striking young woman.

Have I mentioned that Jamey Maxwell has a certain boyish charm? A trait that can be quite becoming in a man, as long as he is not married. Boyish charm can look a lot like premeditated irresponsibility once a man has a wife and children. There is a reason Jamey possesses this youthful appeal. It is almost entirely because of the terrible thing that happened to him on his ninth birthday. Although he survived to live an outwardly normal life, his charm, and I would also say his soul, stopped their evolutionary process on that day. He has retained the essence of a nine-year-old boy.

"Hi, my name is Janette Dean and you look incredibly bored. Mind if I sit down?" she asks with a smile.

"No, please do. And I thought I was hiding my boredom so well. I guess I'm a pretty lousy actor."

"Not really, I was just projecting. Plus, it was a wild guess on my part."

"It's not that I hate parties, it's just that I hate parties that have people at them," Jamey responds, not so jokingly.

"Me too. I am a hopelessly anti-social socialite. A true oxymoron."

"Well, we have something partially in common. I'm a moron…without the oxy."

"I doubt that seriously. Do you have a name?"

"Oh, sorry, I'm Jamey Maxwell. Jamey Maxwell, the socially retarded guest here."

Janette Dean laughs a laugh both sensuous and naive. Jamey likes her already.

"And, I guess I should ask the question all socialites ask new guests: what do you do, Mr. Maxwell?"

"I carve graven images. And you?"

"I worship graven images. But in my spare time I'm a female psychiatrist."

Jamey's smile widens. "Isn't that redundant… female psychiatrist?"

"Yes, I suppose. In my case, however, you could use female as an integer and psychiatrist as a factor of N."

"That's scary," Jamey laughs.

"And what do you do in your spare time, Mr. Maxwell?"

"I consume copious amounts of Miller-Lite. And you can call me Jamey."

"Oh, I prefer to call you Mr. Maxwell. I'm not sure why yet. And if I hear one more positive trait out of you, I will be inclined to propose on the spot. Except for the fact that I'm already married and three months pregnant."

"Yes, we do seem to have things in common, except I'm not married nor am I three months pregnant," Jamey says as he knocks on the wooden coffee table and grins.

"Mr. Boyer tells me you are also an investigator."

"Mr. Boyer is a lousy lying lawyer."

"Now who's being redundant? And, impressively, you're being alliterally redundant. I'm exceedingly impressed. So, will you marry me?"

"Sure. As soon as we kill your husband," Jamey smiles. He doesn't know just how close to prophecy this little joke will become.

Now, here is Jimmy Boyer with the sweetest looking little old lady on his arm. She strongly resembles the cartoon grandmother with which your Tweety Bird lives. Cartoon hair bun and all. And too much white face powder and too much of the red rouge and lipstick which makes most elderly human females look cartoonish. Jimmy, with a somewhat sadistic grin on his face says, "Jamey, I would like you to meet a long-time friend of mine, Mary Nell Chesterfield. She is a San Antonio legend, although she would never admit to it. Among other things, she is the current president of the Daughters of the Tejas Legacy. She also is the godmother of Kristin and Casey. I told her why you are here, aside from enjoying the ambiance."

As Jimmy Boyer completes his introduction, Brad and Vanessa Scofield walk by. Mary Nell Chesterfield, the grand dame of this party, glares at the young Scofields. A specific look Jamey Maxwell has only seen a few times in his life. *Mal de ojo*. The evil eye. If looks could kill then maybe Jamey Maxwell would not have to. But neither life, nor death, is that easy. Dame Chesterfield looks back at Jamey Maxwell with a thin-lipped smile, extends her hand, and says, "Mr. Maxwell."

"My pleasure, Ms. Chesterfield," Jamey offers.

"We will see about that, young man. One thing you may not know is that Kristin was an up and coming member within the Daughters of the Tejas Legacy. I sponsored her and I was grooming her to become an officer. She was such a sweet girl...and very, very intelligent. She would have made a fine president some day. I doubt this has anything to do with her murder. It doesn't seem to be the sort of thing one would kill another over, but this world has become a very strange place, wouldn't you say, Mr. Maxwell? I hope you find what you are looking for here. I would say enjoy the party, but I imagine I would be wasting my breath. Just a note of caution: if, in the course of your investigation, you sully the reputation of my fine organization, to even the slightest degree, I will have your testicles removed. And please do not make the mistake of assuming that I am speaking metaphorically. Have a good evening, Mr. Maxwell."

Jamey produces a small grin, especially compared to the ones on Jimmy Boyer's and Janette Dean's faces, and replies, "You too, ma'am. You too."

When she walks away Jimmy Boyer turns to Jamey Maxwell and says, "That's one fucking cool old lady wouldn't you say, buddy?"

One of the things I have come to love most about the human species: your languages. I am particularly fond of the English language. I would say the same about the Italian language if I happened to be in Italy. But I am not. I am in Texas. I like the colloquialisms. I like the slang. I really like your word 'fuck', with all of its derivatives. So versatile. *Fuck, fucked, fucking, fucker, fuckee, fucky, fucked-up, motherfucker*, et ceteras. It can be a noun, a verb, an adjective, an adverb, an invective, probably even a conjunction, and God knows what else. Angels communicate with each other through intuitive vibrations. Pretty fucking boring, if you get my fucking drift.

After another thirty minutes of long overdue female companionship, Jamey says to Janette Dean, "It's bed-time for Bonzo. In case you were wondering, I'm Bonzo."

"Oh, I knew that. I'm a Bonzo expert. If I were a judge at a Bonzo competition, I'd rate you 'Best of Show'," Janette smiles.

"Thanks. How 'bout lunch tomorrow? I'm buying," Jamey says.

Janette replies, "Sure. Danny's Deli, at the Quarry, 11:00 A.M. Be there or be square."

"Later, gator," says Jamey.

Jamey Maxwell makes his way through the party-goers; says goodnight to Jimmy and Loretta Boyer, says appropriate things to the "hostess with the mostest," and is gone like Elvis.

Back in his hotel room, Jamey Maxwell is in a state of suspended animation. Twilight Zone. Bizarro World.

Dreaming not so sweet dreams. I wish I could help.

He is at the party with Janette Dean. She says, "I really liked meeting you. I think we could make wonderful music together."

"What does that mean?" Jamey asks.

"It means we could torture and kill innocent people 'till the cows come home'," Janette grins grotesquely.

"Please go away," Jamey pleads.

"Never," replies Janette Dean.

Chapter 8

The Seduction

Despite his intention not to get close to another woman for the rest of his unnatural life, Jamey Maxwell finds himself having lunch with Janette Dean. He knows he is setting himself up for disappointment and possibly endangering the well-being of Dr. Dean. But, he is here and she is here and there you are.

Jamey is wearing his party clothes from last night. They worked so well at the shindig…and no use changing horses in mid-stream when you're up shit creek without a saddle. Besides they're the only clothes he brought on the trip, except for his new underwear. He did change those. I think it goes without saying even we Seraphs appreciate that. Janette Dean changed all of her clothes. She is now wearing a white silk blouse, black slacks, black shoes, black purse. Oozing casual class, making it look easy.

Janette Dean is not beautiful. But she is cute as hell, even from a Seraph's point of view. Very short blonde hair. Very blue eyes. Very full lips. And a very odd nose. It's a little too big at the end and a tad crooked.

Remember the Mr. Potato Head toy from your childhood? Well, it looks like someone took the prettiest eyes, lips and hair, and then the most incongruent nose they could find in the toy box, and stuck it on Dr. Dean's head. The result: she is cute as hell, but not beautiful. And, just to add to the effect, someone has set black horn-rimmed glasses on top of that incompatible nose. Here's what Jamey thinks when he looks at her: she's cute as hell. Oh yeah, she also has a nice framework.

Jamey says, "This restaurant is much nicer than I'm used to. Of course, in Dos Cruces there's not a lot to choose from. When I first moved there, I ordered a hamburger at Zenia's Cafe and told the waitress I wanted just mustard on it. Well, after almost an hour, I got a hamburger bun with just mustard on it. No lettuce, no tomato, no meat. But at least I got a bun. I now realize why it took an hour. They were trying to figure out a way to bring me just the mustard. I've learned to be very specific in Dos Cruces."

Janette laughs and says, "I don't think you have to be that specific here, but I wouldn't guarantee it." After a brief pause she adds, "Mr. Maxwell, my professional and personal observations tell me you don't have much of an ego."

Jamey replies, "It was surgically removed years ago. They went in through my rectum." After Janette's laughter subsides, Jamey asks, "So what's it like being a psychiatrist?"

Janette Dean is quiet for a moment, then begins, "You know, many people say psychiatry is nothing more than mental prostitution. You pay for cerebral intercourse…or what they would call in less polite circles, a mind fuck. I have come to consider that a compliment. At least prostitutes perform a public service. In my younger and naiveer days, I would have ranted and raved at anyone who dared to say such a thing. I've seen too much since then, I guess. And I'm only thirty-three years old. Or maybe it's because I haven't been able to save many…or any, of those I consider lost souls. I'm not sure. Maybe one or two. They probably would've saved themselves. So prostitution is a pretty good analogy. But a better one is alchemy. Alchemists, at least the first ones, believed they could turn base metal into gold. As time went by, most of them realized it was a pipe dream. But many of them figured out there was still money to be made…lots of money…and an ample supply of suckers, chumps, and just plain greedy folk willing to buy into pure illusion. So, that's where I now stand on my profession. I'm an alchemist. Pretty pathetic, wouldn't you say?"

Jamey listens and admires.

"I decided to become a psychiatrist after my father committed suicide. I was sixteen. He was forty-four. I loved him so much. So did my mom and my brother. We all worshipped him. Thought he was the smartest person that ever lived. He was so sweet, so kind. He was very successful. An attorney. All of his friends and clients were shocked. Why would someone who had everything kill himself? Mom was not surprised though. She knew someday it would happen. And, deep down, I wasn't surprised. I had seen the darkness sweep over him many times. Usually when things were going well. We would all be around the kitchen table, talking and laughing, and suddenly Dad would disappear. He would be back in his bedroom, sitting in his favorite chair, staring. I would come in and he would immediately act cheerful. He was always joking. I would joke back, but it was all just superficial. Once he detached he couldn't find a way back. I know he wanted to, but…depression is a very cruel disease. And I blame God for letting such a disease exist.

"Anyway, I thought I would become a psychiatrist and save other families…other daughters…other fathers, from suffering such a horrible fate. Loose ends that go on forever. Explanations without merit. Pain without end. My idealism lasted a year or two after graduating from medical school. Not only was I up against depression…there was bipolar disorder, obsessive-compulsive disorder, paranoia, autism, schizophrenia…there are mental illnesses that we don't even have names for yet. For a time I thought drugs, these incredible new and improved medications, would be the answer. I was a true and honest alchemist. These base metal drugs would turn human minds into gold. Oh my. Oh my. My impotence is astounding. My helplessness is off the chart. I'm not sure I can even help myself anymore. I, too, suffer from depression. I, too, have a daughter. And I, too, am unable to protect her from my genes…her genes. She is only five years old and already showing signs of depression. Her name is Eleanor. Ellie. And now I'm bringing another child into this world.

Sex is destruction. This is another thing mankind has never realized. Somehow God sold you a bill of goods that sex is about creation. And in God's frail mind it probably is. So He doesn't even get His own cruelty joke. Think about it — and that shouldn't be a problem with you humans, since you seem to think about it so frequently. But I mean really think about it. Sex is whispered in the shadows, muffled groans and grunts. When you are young it is a dark mystery, vaguely hinted at by those around you. When you get a bit older, your friends let you in on their meager knowledge, although you and they have no idea how meager that knowledge is. False wisdom, twisted humor, and snickers make something dirty of sex and this may be the only truth there is to know: sex is dirty; sex is disgusting.

If you think about sex when you are young, you have sinned. If you have sex out of wedlock, you have sinned. If you have sex with someone other than your spouse, you have sinned. If you have sex with someone of the same sex, you have sinned. And I don't even want to get into incest, bestiality, pedophilia, necrophilia, and other true abominations. Sex is dirty. Sex is disgusting.

Too much sex and you are an addict. Sex offenders are ostracized, jailed, and occasionally chemically castrated. Mentally ill people sometimes cut off their own genitals because they find them repulsive. The Catholic Church forbids sex for its priests and nuns. In ancient days, eunuchs were castrated so they could watch over the king's harem without temptation. Sexual affairs cause divorce. Sexual dysfunction causes affairs. Sex is not to be discussed in polite conversation. Sex destroys lives. Sex destroys love. Sex is destruction.

The act of sex is mostly done in the dark. Many

women, and some men, cannot stand the sight of themselves in the act of sex. Various bodily fluids: semen, mucous, sometimes blood, and God knows what others, are exchanged during the act of sex. And if you have ever witnessed the ultimate aftermath of sex: birth (or creation, as God and you humans are wont to call it), then you have witnessed the violence, the damage. Of course, there is the obvious which humans have ignored from the beginning of their time: life is created to be destroyed. From the moment of birth, the dying begins. Why would God do this?

And with death comes not only the destruction of the life form, but collateral damage to those around it. What kind of mind would invent the act of sex to start with, make most everything about it a sin, and then make such a damaging act the act of creation? You know the answer. Mysterious. Oh yeah, and really fucked up.

Thankfully, we angels were created while God was still sane. There was no sex..., no filth, no destruction involved. We are pure. And we live forever.

Then you have AIDS, gonorrhea, syphilis, chlamydia, genital warts, genital herpes, rape, abortion, sadomasochism, internet porn…shall I continue? No? So tell me how something as dirty, disgusting, and destructive as sex could equal creation. Unless by extrapolation, creation is dirty, disgusting. Unless creation is destruction. Hmmm. Now we're getting somewhere.

To show just how destructive sex is, the angel Azazel and two hundred of our cohorts descended to earth to have sex with women. The result: Nephilim, whom God considers the ultimate abomination.

And, of course, the only reason I am here telling you this story: Kristin Garnett was murdered because Bradley Scofield wanted to have sex with her. Sex is destruction.

"Did you know Billy and Kristin Garnett?" Jamey asks.

"Not Billy, but Kristin. I knew her very well. She was one of my patients." Jamey is not surprised. God had already clued him in on this. Is this why he is here? Maybe. He was hoping he was just here to have lunch with a very cute lady with a sparkling personality.

Dr. Dean continues, "Even though she is dead, I will not share our conversations with you. Besides, there is nothing, no suspects, no reason for her murder, that I could give you. Her problems were of a very personal nature. Self-directed. And as far as I know, from a non-professional standpoint, she didn't have an enemy in the world. I suspect a random act of violence."

Then out of nowhere, the bombshell: "Mr. Maxwell, my husband beats me."

Jamey Maxwell remains silent. Quiet seems right.

"We met in medical school. We were both interns at the UT Health Science Center. Robert was handsome, and superficial, two traits I was looking for at the time. Don't ask why. He seemed harmless enough. As soon as we finished our residencies, we married. Within two months, he was shoving me, berating me. Within three months, the beatings began. He was smart enough to hit me where the bruises wouldn't be apparent to others. My stomach, my breasts, my thighs. Within two years, Ellie came. During the pregnancy and after she came, the beatings stopped for a while. For a few months, he was caught up in fatherhood. But he got over it. We've been married seven years now. Oh yes, after he beats me, he always tells me I'm ugly.

"I'm pregnant again. But it hasn't stopped him this time. In fact, the beatings come more often now. He's really angry. He does not want this child. I'm not sure I do either.

"You're probably wondering why I've stayed in this situation. Mr. Maxwell, I know you will understand this. I know a lot about you. I know about your murder case in Dos Cruces. It made the papers here in San Antonio. I know about your family. People talk. And I know you suffer from depression. Don't forget, I'm a female psychiatrist. We're omniscient." Janette Dean laughs. A sad laugh.

"And that's the answer…depression, I mean. Depression is paralyzing. It makes you afraid to make decisions. You assume whatever you do will only make things worse. It's physically exhausting. You don't have the energy or the confidence to do the right thing. It's a disease you don't want to talk about with others. It's kind of like a very cranky friend of mother's said when my mom asked if she had seen a picture of my mom's new granddaughter. The friend said, "No, and I appreciate it." That's how people feel when you don't talk to them about depression. They appreciate it.

"I've never shared this with anyone. Not my mother. Not my brother. I think they suspected something was wrong between Robert and me, but they would have been stunned to hear he beat me.

"Of course, they knew I suffered from depression.

It's genetic. And last one out of the gene pool is 'it', as my brother liked to kid me. That's the only way he knew how to relate to it. We both, fortunately, inherited my Dad's sense of humor. Anyway, I never talked about depression with them. With my Dad's suicide, they had reached their depression quota. Would you like another cup of depression? Oh no, thanks, we've had plenty. All of that is a moot point now. My brother died in a car wreck two years ago and my mother died of cancer a year ago last month. She actually died as soon as she heard my brother had been killed, but her body lived on a while longer. Life so very sucks.

"So you see, you're the lucky one. You've drawn the Old Maid. I've decided to share all of these fun facts with you. And I've only known you for two days. Go figure." Janette smiles a lonely smile, accompanied by a tear.

Jamey reaches across the small table, takes both of her hands, looks into her eyes, and says, "You are right about me, of course. I've suffered from depression since I was a child. Since I was nine. As I grew older, I fancied I was overcoming all of it. Actually I was finding incredibly selfish ways to mask the symptoms. Then I lost my family. And since then, there's not a day that goes by that I don't think about killing myself.

"Look at me, Janette. I will be your friend. I will listen to you. I will do anything in my power to help you. But never, ever, tell me or anyone else that you do not want your baby. Because I refuse to believe it's true. In a perfect world, there would be no such thing as depression. But this world is about as far from perfect, without actually being Hell, as you can get. And the only thing…the only thing…we have going for us here on Earth is love. I'm not talking about so-called romantic love. I'm talking about the love between parents and children. And, especially, the love a mother has for her baby. That's as close to perfection as we get in this world. Don't fuck it up."

Janette Dean quietly sobs. People at the next table glance sideways, believing they are being inconspicuous.

"While you have a good cry, I'm going to tell you something that will make you forget about your troubles and, quite possibly, make you get up and run for the exit." Jamey winks at her. "I have this thing…this thing about pregnant women. I think they're sexy. And not in a generic way. Not like you say, wow, that Lexus is sexy. Or that purse is sexy. I mean sexually desirable. I mean I want to have sex with them. All of them. Yes, even the ugly ones, which does not include you, in spite of what your husband says. Now there are so many things wrong with this, I try not to think about it. You would think males, even human males, would stop thinking about a female once his, or someone else's job, is done. Evolution should dictate that one should move on at this point and find other flowers to pollinate. At least, mentally. You don't see many men's magazines with a pregnant woman occupying the centerfold. But with me, it's the opposite. Some form of de-evolution, I guess. The more pregnant a woman gets, the sexier she gets. When I see a lady who's nine months pregnant, my testosterone level maxes out. Like a cartoon thermometer. Since you're only three months pregnant, you're relatively safe. You're not even showing yet. But I'm not sure how long my platonic feelings toward you will last."

By this time, Janette's tears are gone and she is giggling. "I'll take my chances." She looks at Jamey with a sly grin, shaking her head. "Do you realize what a find you are, Mr. Maxwell? You are the missing link that women have been searching for. The holy grail of manhood. The one that Oprah, and Cosmopolitan, and the Oxygen network have been talking about all these years. But they never knew exactly what the perfect man really is. And now here you are. The perfect man is the one who thinks even ugly pregnant women are sexually attractive. I feel like I've found Bigfoot and the Loch Ness Monster rolled into one. I've found the most mythical creature of all. And I'm not letting him go. You thought my proposal last night was a joke. Well, last night it was. Today I'm serious. You must marry me."

"I'm better as a theory," Jamey replies. "Or as they say, I look good on paper. I wouldn't pawn myself off on my worst enemy. And certainly not on a pretty little thing like you."

Now that the conversation has stabilized, Janette and Jamey talk about other less traumatic, but no less fun and interesting, topics for the next hour and a half. Neither one of them wants this lunch to end, but finally it must. However they agree to meet again for lunch tomorrow, same time, same station.

Jamey Maxwell is asleep in his motel room. He is again dreaming of his girls, Julie and Josie. They are little. Two and four years old. They are beautiful. They are speaking as teenagers. "Dad, we miss you. When are you coming home?"

Jamey says, "Soon…soon."

It's the next day. Jamey meets Janette Dean at the same little bistro. This time Ellie is with her. Janette gives Jamey that "I'm sorry, couldn't help it" look. Ellie's babysitter had failed to show up. Jamey doesn't mind. It's been a while since he has been around a young child, a young girl. He thinks of his Julie and his Josie.

"Ellie, this is Mr. Maxwell, a friend of mine," Janette says.

Jamey smiles at Ellie and says, "It is a pleasure to make your acquaintance, Ellie. And how are you today?"

Ellie studies Jamey for a moment and replies, "Fine, thank you. Do you love my mommy?"

Janette, surprised and flustered, scolds her daughter, "Ellie, what kind of question is that? You're being rude."

Jamey intervenes, "It's a perfectly fine question and I don't consider it rude. Ellie, your mother is very nice, very pretty, and very smart. I've only known her for a short time and I like her very much. We are just good friends."

"That didn't answer my question," Ellie replies.

"Well, how about this? I don't know. But it would not be right for me to love your mom since she's married to your father," Jamey says.

"My mommy and daddy fight sometimes."

"Ellie! Stop it. This is so…wrong…and embarrassing," Janette struggles.

"It's okay, Janette, let Ellie talk. I think she needs to."

Jamey turns to Ellie and asks, "What do you think when your mom and dad fight?"

"I think I want a new daddy. One that isn't so mean."

Janette has given up on trying to stop her daughter from expressing herself. Jamey seems to be capable of handling this conversation.

"Well, Ellie, it's not that easy to get a new daddy. Maybe your daddy is just a little broken and needs to be fixed," Jamey suggests. He is profoundly moved by the depth of emotions emanating from this most precocious five year old. One of the emotions not emanating is joy. It makes Jamey Maxwell very sad.

"My daddy is mean, not broken. My mommy needs to divorce him," states Ellie. "Do you have kids?"

"Well, yes, I have two daughters."

"Where are they?" Ellie asks.

"They passed away a long time ago."

"You mean they're dead?"

Tears suddenly appear in Jamey Maxwell's eyes, and he answers, "Yes, they're dead."

"How did they die?"

"In a car wreck, along with their mother."

"So you're not married now?" Ellie is doing the math.

"No, Ellie."

"You're kinda weird," Ellie offers. This seems unrelated to the present conversation, but Jamey doubts that. "And you're kinda old. That's okay, I guess."

Ellie, having made her point about Jamey Maxwell, and having endured adult conversation much too long, is getting restless. She makes this point perfectly clear to her mother. Janette and Jamey say hasty goodbyes and agree to meet again the next time he is in the city.

Jamey heads to his depressing motel. He makes his way to his room and crashes on top of the dirty bedspread covering a worn-out queen size mattress.

In his dream, Jamey is back at St. Charles Place. His daughters, Julie and Josie are sitting with him on his old, dirty couch. They have their arms around him. They love him so.

Josie says, "Daddy, there's something wrong. I don't know what it is, but I just know it."

Julie says, "Be careful, Daddy. Someone wants to hurt you. Really bad."

Jamey looks in the kitchen and sees a legless man next to the little gas stove, sitting on the floor. The old, dissheveled man is grinning at him.

This is all so wrong. In so many ways.

Chapter 9

The Sensation

God's messages are getting more confusing to Jamey Maxwell. What they lack in clarity, however, they make up for in volume. The messages are coming non-stop now, and Jamey is no longer sure if they are actually from God or someone even more sinister. Or, he thinks, maybe he has blown past major depressive disorder, and gone directly to schizophrenia. Jamey is not doing well at all. He hates motel rooms.

Jamey is thinking about his lost family and his guilt. And he has discovered this secret of life: taking others for granted, especially loved ones, is not an act of betrayal. It is a biological necessity. No human can just love and love and love, all the time. And neither can angels, really. There must be down time. Jamey Maxwell knows this now. For he so misses his Connie Lee and Julie and Josie that every thought of them causes the love to ooze to the surface. An abscess that never really heals. The infection is pure. The infection is painful. The infection is terminal. He wishes he could just take them for granted again. Like he did when they were alive.

Do you think God created the universe as a metaphor for Himself? That is probably the number one topic of discussion amongst us Seraphs. The general consensus is "yes." The metaphor, of course, being emptiness. What other explanation could there possibly be for such a vast, empty creation? The universe, that is...and God too, for that matter. And we're not talking about just the emptiness of the cosmos. What about the emptiness within every particle of matter that exists? Have you ever seen a diagram of a molecule? Aren't molecules virtually empty spheres with thin outer crusts of some sort? Aren't humans and everything else on Earth made of molecules? Even we angels are molecularly constructed beings, with considerably more amorphous capabilities, of course.

If God wasn't seeking a metaphor, why would He waste so much space? Or so much time and effort? Why would He fill every living, and non-living, thing with empty atoms and molecules? Why not just make a spleen a spleen? No empty molecules or wasted space! Just a fucking spleen! And what does a fucking spleen do anyway? Jesus! And did you know that the molecules of the human body are completely replaced every two or three months? So every two or three months, you, my friend, are a completely different physical being. The next time you say, "I'm not myself today," it should have a new, significant meaning.

And what about the true emptiness in this world: the emptiness of the human mind, the human heart, the human spirit, the human soul? It's pretty fucking hard to keep all of those containers filled, right? Iraq, Bosnia, Afghanistan, Somalia, North Korea, Iran, genocide, terrorism, starvation, nuclear blackmail. So what in the hell is all this about? Maybe, it is about Hell. Hell is immeasurably more empty than the universe, or Heaven, or God. Fuck it, I don't know. It's all too confusing, even for us virtually empty angels.

The messages seem to be telling Jamey to go somewhere and talk to someone. "Now that's specific," he says to himself. He has already planned on going to Langtry and Sandersville to begin his investigation, but the communiqués indicate he will encounter mysteries and mysterious beings. God is being his usual helpful Self. God never gives Jamey Maxwell the big picture, *la imagen grande,* because He knows Jamey would want to inflict grievous harm upon himself...and God too, if given the chance.

But before beginning his trip to West Texas with all its potential mysteries, Jamey has a little matter to settle with a certain assholish, pregnant spouse-abusing psychiatrist. He picks up the phone and makes an appointment. And how fortunate, there has been a cancellation at the doctor's office and they can work James St. Michael in at 9:00 in the morning.

Hours pass. Jamey is tired; weary. He performs some perfunctory hygiene measures, crawls into his hotel bed and prepares for another night of nightmares, mostly of the waking variety.

"I met this young woman that I'm very fond of. She's married — to an asshole that abuses her."

"I see. And how does that make you feel?"

"Well, sometimes at night, when I'm standing in the bedroom doorway, watching the two of them sleeping, I want to pull out my Model 59 and shoot the guy in the balls. But I don't because I'm afraid that it will upset her. I'm afraid it will wake up their young daughter. And did I mention that she's pregnant? The gutless bastard abuses a pregnant woman and the mother of his child. Can you believe it?"

Dr. Dean begins to turn a whiter shade of pale. "And w-what does that have to do with God?"

By this time, it appears Jamey Maxwell is no longer listening to Dr. Dean. He is continuing to describe his feelings. "So instead of shooting the prick, I decide to slit his throat with the knife I use to carve my little angels and saints with. That way it will make very little noise and he won't be able to scream…so it won't wake her up. Did I mention that she's a psychiatrist and she's married to a psychiatrist? The bastard that's doing this is a fucking psychiatrist. Can you believe it? Anyway, after I slit his throat I was gonna castrate him real fast and show him his balls as he's choking on his blood. But then I worried this would upset her; to wake up with blood all over her clean sheets. She likes to keep a neat house, you see."

Jamey continues, "Anyway, this isn't what God wanted; too easy, too fast, not enough pain. I'm telling you, He's really pissed. So I wait 'til the next night and the sleazy son-of-a-bitch calls her and tells her he's working late. He's working alright. Working on his cute little receptionist. So I follow them to her place and when they're done with their fornicating, I stand in the bedroom doorway and watch them sleeping, and God's telling me 'remember what you did to *Los Diablos*? It's time.'"

Dr. Dean, on the verge of losing all of his bodily functions, interrupts, "Y-you mean you've hurt people before?"

"Killed them actually. Only three, *Los Diablos*. And they weren't merely dead, they were most sincerely dead. They deserved it, I think. At least God thought so. He really hated them."

"I-I see. And what do you think it would take for God not to be so angry with this new person, this psychiatrist?"

"Oh, that's easy, God told me that if this feces-eating *marrano* would pack his bags and move to Dallas within the next twenty-four hours, and then file for divorce within the next five business days. Well, that would pretty well take care of it as far as He's concerned." With that, the thirty-minute session timer bell goes off, prematurely. Dr. Whitley farts and jumps from his chair.

Jamey Maxwell, as if waking from a trance, says, "Well Doc, I guess time's up. You know, I feel much better now. I don't think I will need to be seeing you again, huh Doc?"

"No, Mr. St. Michael, you won't need to see me again. And don't worry about your bill. It's taken care of," Dean says as he opens his office door.

Christina looks at Dr. Dean with that deer-in-the-headlight look. Dr. Dean looks at Christina with the look of a man who just crapped his pants.

Part III

The Investigation

Chapter 1

Wisdom of the Santero

Jamey Maxwell is back in Dos Cruces after his little adventure in San Antonio, including his pep talk with a certain spouse-abusing psychiatrist. He has delayed his trip to West Texas, opting for a day of R and R and R, rest, recuperation, and reception of copious amounts of Miller-Lite. Unfortunately, the beer doesn't affect him anymore, except in the abstract. It's just a habit and a routine. And Jamey Maxwell values routine to an extraordinary degree. It's the only thing that keeps him from floating away, or blowing his brains out. After his one day hiatus, he is now back at Miguel Vera's workshop. Another newfound routine. Miguel, the *santero*. Miguel, the saintmaker. Miguel, Jamey Maxwell's savior.

Miguel is old. At least eighty. And everything about him looks older than that, except for his eyes. His dark brown skin has turned to leather. It is accentuated by a shock of white hair on top his semi-ancient head. His misshapen hands are scarred from years of mishaps with his carving tools. But Miguel has the twinkling brown eyes of a five-year-old boy. The twinkling masks the fact that Miguel has felt no joy in many years (since 1964 to be exact). The twinkling also masks the fact that the light in the old man's eyes is fading. Miguel Veras is going blind. Cataracts, ptyregiums and a life lived in sacrifice are conspiring to destroy his vision; the destruction soon to be complete. But not his inner vision. Miguel has the mind of a prophet, a poet, and an artist and he is all of these things. Jamey loves the old man. The old man loves Jamey.

After the deaths of so many people close to him: his beloved father, St. Charles; his beautiful wife and daughters, Connie Lee, Julie and Josie; *la innocenta* Angelita; brave little Marisol Cortinas; after all of these deaths, Jamey began his search for a reason to exist. His search did not take him far from his home at St. Charles Place in Dos Cruces. On the other side of the railroad tracks, less than a quarter of a mile away, he found Miguel Vera and his reason to exist. So after a year of nightly prayers that went like this, "Dear God, please kill me. Amen," Jamey found reprieve. Reprieve, however, can be brief "on Earth as it is in Heaven."

Jamey Maxwell had heard about the old *santero* from the time he moved to Dos Cruces. But since Miguel Vera did not hang out at Zenia's place, drinking, and since Jamey Maxwell did not hang out at the Catholic church, praying, their paths never crossed. Which is hard to believe, Dos Cruces being such a tiny village. Maybe the timing had to be just right.

One day, *con desesperación y sin esperanza*, Jamey Maxwell walked from St. Charles Place to Miguel Veras' studio. As he approached he could see through the large windows. The old man was inside, carving.

Jamey knocked on the door. Miguel, never one to hurry even when he was young, slowly made it to the door. "*Diga,*" Miguel said with a wry smile. Jamey had a feeling the old man had been waiting for him for years.

"*Señor* Veras, my name is Jamey Maxwell."

"*Sí,* I know who you are. *Dos Cruces es muy pequeña, verdad?*"

Jamey Maxwell grinned, "*Seguro que sí.*"

"Come inside. *Bienvenido,*" said the old *santero.*

Thus began the unlikely yet preordained friendship.

The *santero* tradition is ancient. As long as there have been religions on this earth there have been *santeros. Santeros* make saints for the poor. Rich people could always afford the finest artists: Michelangelo, Raphael, Giotto, to carve and paint saints for them. The less privileged had to rely on *santeros* to make their religious icons. Saintmaking is folk art in its purest form.

The *santero* custom came to Texas and the Southwest with the Spanish explorers and flourished in the eighteenth and nineteenth centuries. Since then, it has survived in isolated pockets in New Mexico and Texas. And, irony of ironies, what began as a noble craft for the poor has turned into an idle and/or idol avocation for the rich. Much to the dismay of true *santeros,* in New Mexico it has become a commercial venture. Wealthy collectors come to Santa Fe from all over the world to buy religious folk art, both antique and new. Selling saints for profit is considered blasphemy by most traditional saintmakers, and this is true of Miguel Veras. He believes his carvings and paintings are meant to be used, exclusively, for religious purposes.

Jamey Maxwell, grieving, became Miguel's apprentice almost a year ago. At first, his job was to sharpen the chisels, adzes, and knives; oil the round wooden mallets; and keep the workshop clean and orderly. After a few months, Miguel began to teach Jamey to carve. In New Mexico, artists traditionally use cottonwood roots for their carvings. There are virtually no cottonwood trees in South Texas, so Miguel uses mesquite roots. Mesquite roots are gnarly and reddish brown in color, much like Miguel Veras' arthritic hands. Mesquite is also one of the hardest woods known to man or as Jamey Maxwell likes to say, "mesquite is harder than Chinese algebra." Because the wood is so hard, the carving tools have to be sharpened frequently. So even though Jamey is now carving, his main job is still to keep Miguel's tools in good condition. For most people this would be a monotonous chore, but for Jamey, oiling the tools and working them on the whetstone is to lose himself for a while, and therefore to lose his grief for a while. He needs the respite. Now that Miguel allows Jamey to carve after tool duties are finished, he can lose himself even more.

Jamey Maxwell's first carving was *Santa Lucía*, an early saint whose eyes were gouged out before being martyred. She is traditionally depicted holding a platter in her hand. On the platter are her two eyeballs. There are several subliminal reasons Jamey picked Saint Lucy as his first carving, not the least being Miguel's inevitable blindness. For a first carving, the results were quite good. Primitive but not crude. Jamey Maxwell has a God-given (literally speaking) talent for the *santero* vocation.

Jamey gets to the workshop by 6:00 A.M. and always

finds Miguel carving. The thousand-square-feet workshop is a work of art in itself. It is made of adobe bricks and the inside walls are white plaster. Miguel's workbench is an old butcher block, eight feet long, that he found in Mexico many years ago. The floor is handmade clay tile produced by Miguel himself. During daylight hours, all of this is illuminated by sunlight coming through oversized wooden windows salvaged from an abandoned grocery store. In the pre-dawn and at night, fluorescent lights are necessary. The plaster walls are lined with tools, hundreds of them, neatly organized. Miguel insists on this. And on the many wooden shelves are Miguel's carvings, in various states of completion. The overall effect is that of an expensive art gallery in Santa Fe.

In the winter, Miguel has the old fifty-five gallon drum stove fired up with mesquite scraps when Jamey arrives. The smell is wonderful and the heat from the stove and the quiet affection from Miguel warm Jamey's soul. There is coffee sitting on the wood stove and it is delicious.

It is almost summer now, so the wood stove is dormant. But Miguel's warmth and the good coffee are there. Daniel Galvan, the goatboy, shows up at 7 A.M. escorted by Taz, the part blue healer, part inexplicable, one-eyed wonderdog. Daniel is Jamey Maxwell's best friend. Daniel is a mass of tousled black hair and smiling crooked yellow teeth. He helps Miguel and Jamey keep the workshop clean. So, the three humans: the old *santero*, the retired Customs agent, and *un muchacho retardado*, begin a day of creating Christian artifacts. The continuation of a ritual begun over two millennia ago. Taz watches.

Since Jamey is a man of few words, Miguel a man of even fewer words, and Daniel a man of virtually no words, the conversations are sparse, but full of nuance. And always full of significance. The significance is life itself. Miguel Veras has outlived his wife and three sons. Jamey Maxwell has outlived everyone close to him except for Jimmy Boyer, Miguel, and Daniel. And Daniel Galvan is truly a lost soul who has been found. So, amidst the aftermath of so much death and sorrow, these three men choose life. They choose to create.

And the creations are magnificent. Miguel is an exceptional artist by any standard. His carvings of *La Virgen de Guadalupe* are legendary. His crucifixes inspire people to kneel on the spot and genuflect. His carved saints, *San José*, *San Antonio*, *San Pedro*, all of the others, have miracles attributed to them. Patrons come from Laredo, San Antonio, Monterrey, even Mexico City, to purchase his carvings and his paintings. But he does not sell to everyone. He must be convinced that his saints are to be used for religious purposes only. He prefers to sell only to people of modest means. He carves saints for Catholic churches throughout the southwest for free. And despite all of this, most of his carvings eventually wind up in the hands of wealthy collectors. Miguel Veras knows this, but never discusses it.

This morning Jamey arrives earlier than usual. He did not sleep well. Investigating the murders of Billy and Kristin Garnett has resurrected the ghosts. They come to Jamey every night now. They speak to him. They speak of love. They speak of loneliness. They speak of broken promises and unfulfilled dreams. If he were not already insane, they would drive him there. Miguel is one of the few people who realizes Jamey Maxwell *está loco como una cabra*. Crazy as a bed bug. He loves Jamey even more because of it.

"*Buenos días, Jaime. Cómo está*?" asks Miguel.

"*Así, así*," Jamey replies.

"The dreams?"

"Yes, they're getting worse."

"*Es por trabajar en las muertes*. You must stop. Let *la policía* do their work. You must stay and make the saints and become crazy like me. *Los locos de Dos Cruces, verdad*?" Miguel slyly smiles and his ancient brown eyes sparkle. Jamey wishes he could stay here with Miguel and Daniel, but he knows God will not let him.

"Miguel, what do you know about vinegaroons?"

"*No entiendo*," he replies. "Say it in Spanish."

"*Alacranes del diablo*," Jamey says. "Devil scorpions. They were found all over the two bodies."

Miguel looks at Jamey and for a moment the old man's eyes look primordial, and very tired. "Ahh," Miguel sighs and then becomes quiet. He closes his eyes and appears to be sleeping. With his eyes still closed Miguel whispers, "*Dios esté con él y lo proteja.*"

Miguel opens his eyes and begins, "Jaime, you must be very careful. *Cuidado*. You walk with evil. God gives you this sign. It is a warning. *Muy peligroso.* Very dangerous. *Por favor*, stay with me *aquí* in Dos Cruces. Do not look at these things anymore." Of course, Miguel knows this plea is fruitless. He knows Jamey will not listen.

"Miguel, you must tell me what you know. I need to know."

"*Bueno*," Miguel, with resignation, begins, "There are stories, very old stories, about the devil scorpion. *Mi Viejo*, my grandfather, showed me the way of the *santero*. He showed me how to clean the workshop, sharpen the tools, smooth the wood, rub oil on the mesquite to make it *más* beautiful. He showed me many things, Jaime. *Una vez, nada más,* he told me the story of *alacranes del diablo*. He told me this just one time, and he spoke softly and sadly. It was a warning. He said, 'Miguelito, you have seen the devil scorpion. God sent this scorpion to Earth to find the evil ones. These *alacranes* are the…*cómo se llama*?…guards. They watch for the devil and his *compadres*. Do not fear them, *pero*, do not seek them out. It is said that when they find the evil ones, they will attack. They will use their poison to blind and to kill. They will show no mercy. God willing, you will never see, *no mirarás*, such a thing. And never again will I speak of this to you.'"

Miguel continues, "I am very afraid for you, Jaime. *Tengo mucho miedo*."

Insanity. Have I mentioned that all of you humans are insane to one degree or another? What I have yet to understand is why you fight insanity — why you fear it? It is a most precious resource. A treasure that goes unmined. Consider this: you spend your dreadful lives trying to succeed at something, anything, but success is rarely achieved. Or if it is achieved then you strive to succeed at something else. And even though you all are going to die anyway, this striving is killing you. In the end what have you accomplished? Money? Fame?

Some sort of ephemeral legacy? In the end, all of this striving (and the soiled fruit of this striving) is forgotten. Have you ever been inside a psychiatric ward, an insane asylum, a feeb factory, a silly circus, a nuthouse, a funny farm? No? Then let me tell you this: those confined are confined only physically. Mentally, they are free to explore the universe, as well as Heaven and Hell. They do not strive to succeed, for that pressure does not exist in their world. They live. That's what they do. They live for a nanosecond and they live for an eternity. And this they do a thousand times each day. They are virtually immortal. Insanity is one of God's greatest gifts to humans…and the most unappreciated.

Just a warning: insanity is as close to immortality as most humans, if they knew what awaited them, would want to attain.

Daniel and Taz arrive at 7:00 A.M., as usual. Both have grins on their faces. Taz is an unusual canine, to say the least. Unlike most dogs, who seem to us Watchers to be perpetually happy, his countenance actually reflects his mood. When Taz is of a bad humor, everyone knows it. He can frown just as effectively as he can smile. Most of the time he wears a slight sneer. This is how he generally views the world. With benign contempt.

Daniel is just the opposite. He is unable to project any outward emotion other than joy. His grin is permanent. It is a reflection of his beautiful soul and it is his one and only defense mechanism. Isn't it sad that a person with a beautiful soul must have a defense mechanism? Particularly one so ineffective. Such is life on your planet Earth.

Back at St. Charles Place, the phone rings. Jamey Maxwell answers.

"Mr. Maxwell, my husband has left me," says Janette Dean.

"I'm sorry to hear that, I guess."

"You're a very poor liar. So am I, so I won't. I'm relieved. It does strike me as quite a coincidence, though. Just a couple of days ago I was telling you about my husband and our situation and then all of a sudden he ups and leaves. Is it a coincidence, Mr. Maxwell?"

Silence. And then, "Well, since I'm such a lousy liar, I'll just plead the Fifth," says Jamey Maxwell.

"Okay. I must tell you, aside from being momentarily relieved, I'm not sure how I feel about this yet. I'm not going to say thank you. Not at this time. Maybe soon. Maybe never. I just don't know. I'm also not going to say you should've minded your own business. There's a reason I told you our story. So, at this point, it's as much my fault as yours. I may even be grateful some day, but I'm not yet. And I know it's a contradiction to say I'm glad he's left but I'm not thankful to you. My feelings are ambiguous to say the least. I know I'm starting to ramble, so I will go now. I'll call you soon. Or not." With that, Dr. Janette Dean hangs up the phone.

Jamey Maxwell holds the phone to his ear for a few moments longer. And here is why: he actually thinks if he keeps the receiver to his ear for just a while, he might hear the voice of his dead wife or one of his dead daughters. He thinks he might hear one of them say,

"It's okay now." As usual, he is wrong.

Sitting on his old beat-up couch, fatigue finally overcomes Jamey Maxwell. He dozes off.

In a dream Connie says, "Be careful. Someone is trying to hurt you. Like you hurt us. Remember?"

"I didn't mean to," replies Jamey.

"That's what they all say," Connie says with a smile.

Chapter 2

The Come On Inn

Jamey Maxwell is drawing nearer. He is now leaving Del Rio headed for Sandersville, county seat of Torres County. He finds that he has an overwhelming thirst, even greater than usual, for an ice cold Miller-Lite longneck. He sees the sign for the Come On Inn and decides he must pull over. I hear him open the door of his old beat-up blue truck. He closes the driver door. I hear his footsteps crunching the gravel. He opens the front door of the Come On Inn.

"Hey cowboy, how's it hangin'?" I ask.

"To the left, as always," he answers.

Twenty-three men sitting at booths, tables, and the bar, stop their assorted conversations to stare at Jamey Maxwell. I told you earlier that I chose my incarnation on earth as a woman living in a trailer park in Del Rio and working as a barmaid at the Come On Inn. What I didn't tell you is that I chose, for now, to look like Claudia Schieffer, the German supermodel. If I were dressed only in my underwear and had soft, white feathery wings sprouting from my back, as you humans like to picture us angels, I would look just like

Claudia in one of her Victoria's Secret commercials. If you saw the real me, a Seraph, you would fall to the ground and choke on your own vomit. Enoch described us as "fiery serpents having six wings and four heads." Enoch didn't have a clue.

Jamey looks around at all the men, mostly younger than him, and says, "I can't believe the county fire marshal hasn't shut you down for occupancy overload."

"That's him at the end of the bar over there," I say, pointing to the county official. The fire marshal turns various shades of red for various reasons.

Jamey looks at him and asks, "Do you believe in spontaneous combustion?" Jamey gets no answer. He can tell the testosterone fumes are rising.

"How 'bout I bring you a cold Miller-Lite, darlin'?"

"You read my mind, sweetheart," Jamey replies.

So with twenty-three jaws, and penises, at half-mast and twenty-three sets of eyes glaring holes through Jamey Maxwell, I bring him a cold beer. And to up the ante I say, "scoot over, lover boy," slide into the booth beside him and give him a big kiss on the cheek. I have worked at the Come On Inn for exactly one week. The clientele has grown from one old fart to an additional twenty-two males gathered together in holy lustimony. Almost all of them married. The most they have heard come from my lips is "What can I get you?" and "Thanks." The testosterone fumes are approaching ignition point. Spontaneous combustion is a distinct possibility. This is fun.

Monogamy. When it comes to monogamy, you humans are so hardheaded. Especially female humans. God gives you the answer to whether monogamy is possible, or even desirable. He plasters the evidence throughout your planet. He shoves it in your face. And, yet, you ignore. The answer — the overwhelming evidence — is the world around you. Check it out. Animal life. Have you ever seen a male dog whispering sweet nothings in a female dog's ear, promising to be ever faithful, while humping away, hurrying to ejaculate, so he can move on to fuck the next bitch? Plant life. Plants get gangbanged daily by bees and various insects. And the plants like it. A lot. I suspect if rocks could move, they too would be promiscuous. It's God's plan. What the fuck else do you need to see? Oh, yeah, check out human life too. Open your eyes, look around. Now, how well do you think monogamy's working? Be honest. God hates liars.

"Do I know you?" Jamey asks.

"No, but I know you," I reply.

And now I begin to speak in a language, a form of ancient Aramaic, neither Jamey nor anyone at this bar, nor any human alive on this planet for that matter, has ever heard spoken. I will speak this way for the next fifteen minutes and Jamey will be surprised to know that he not only understands this language but also speaks it fluently, at least for the next fifteen minutes. And then he will forget that he ever met a beautiful young barmaid at the Come On Inn on the outskirts of Del Rio or that he had ever even visited this establishment. And the other twenty-three occupants of the Come On Inn will find that for the remainder of their days on Earth they will have a fifteen minute hole in their lives which will never be filled.

Jamey Maxwell leaves the Come On Inn in a haze.

He manages to find a motel room at Lake Amistad. He makes it to his room, falls into bed with all of his clothes on, and slips into a deep sleep.

Jamey Maxwell is sitting in Zenia's Place, talking to Marisol Cortinas and Angelita Cavazos. They are both dead.

Marisol says, "Mister, you are such a mess. What are you going to do now?"

Angelita laughs liltingly, "Yeah, Jaime, now what? You can't just sit here drinking, can you?"

This is so unfair to Jamey. He is still struggling to survive. I wish they would leave him alone. But I doubt that they will.

He just pulls a swig from his Miller-Lite and listens to the girls. They look so beautiful. Long dark brown hair, deep brown eyes, olive skin. They could be mother and daughter.

"Don't worry about us. We're fine now," says Marisol.

"Yeah, at least I got the hell out of D.C.," adds Angelita.

Marisol inquires, "Have you talked to your wife and daughters lately? I bet they miss you terribly."

"You were such a good father," Angelita says.

Jamey Maxwell takes another sip of *cerveza* and begins to cry.

Human dreams are often so cruel and pointless.

Chapter 3

The Three Stooges and a Texas Ranger

Enlightened by his visit with me, but totally oblivious from whence came his newfound knowledge of apocrypha, including The Book of Enoch, Jamey Maxwell heads for Sandersville. He intends to meet with the law enforcement officials of Torres County. All three of them. The Three Stooges as they are semi-affectionately known locally. They, along with Texas Ranger Earl McVay, are investigating the murders of Kristin and Billy Garnett. They do not know Jamey is coming. He prefers it that way. He likes to surprise people.

Between Dunedin and Sandersville, which is literally nowhere, a vacant place in the universe, Jamey Maxwell sees an old man on the side of the road. The codger is sitting. Just sitting. He looks a lot like a character actor from your old western movies: Gabby Hayes. Grizzled. Very very grizzled. Jamey Maxwell stops and backs up. For a brief moment I hate Jamey Maxwell. I have always hated the old man.

When Jamey pulls up beside this, this man, he understands why *el vejarrón* is just sitting. Gabby-fucking-Hayes has no legs. He probably did at one time. I do not remember now. I have a mental block, a blind spot when it comes to him. God's doing of course. I do not give a rat's ass or a flying fuck. Or a flying fucking rat's ass.

Jamey realizes he has seen the old man before, but cannot remember where. He wonders to himself, How in the hell could I forget a legless old man? Jamey shakes it off.

"Where you headed?" Jamey asks.

"Who said I was headed anywhere?" replies the old geezer with the voice from a realm that no longer exists. If it ever did. Then he smiles. He has a perfect set of sparkling teeth. They are real. He, though, is not.

"Well just thought you might need a lift." Jamey is now captivated. Mesmerized. I will not say hypnotized for that is just a cheap human trick.

"I get around just fine. I'm here ain't I?" The old man seems to be vibrating. Jamey thinks he is seeing things. I know better.

"You from around here somewhere?"

"I suppose you could say that. Especially the somewhere part." The old man is playing a game which is not a game. His magic is strong. Did I mention that I hated him? It is a long story I think; about another place and another time and it escapes me and I do not really care except I would like the old man to disappear but he is not really there so that is an impossibility.

"Need some water? Or a Miller-Lite?" Jamey asks.

"Nope. I doubt you have anything I need. But I have something you need."

"Oh? What's that?" Jamey feels the hammer begin to

fall.

"I have a message from your wife and daughters," the old man replies.

All the joy of the past, memories, but only the good memories of his beloved girls, instantly flood Jamey's senses. The first time he laid eyes on his Connie Lee. The first time he laid eyes on his sweet and fragile Julie. The first time he laid eyes on Josie, full of the secrets of life. The dance recitals; the t-ball games; the kindergarten graduations; the first boyfriends; making love to his Connie Lee and seeing her smile, the one she saved for only him; eclectic visions, but not random ones. Jamey is crying now. Tears of joy, tears of solace, tears of reprieve. When he regains his composure, he opens his mouth to speak to the old man. But the old man, of course, is gone. I am glad.

Throughout my myriad millennia on earth, I have born witness to countless atrocities and countless miracles and all that lies between. The common denominator in all of these events is humans. I have seen the worst mankind has had to offer: the Egyptian Pharaoh Akhenaton, the Roman Emperor Caligula, the German Führer Adolph Hitler, and many lesser megalomaniacs. I have also seen the radiance mankind has somehow been able to produce: Socrates, Jesus Christ (yes, he was a man), Albert Schweitzer, Mother Teresa. But what draws me and other Watchers closer to humans is not the extremes of the spectrum, but the dignity in which your everyday people, your "average Joes and Joanns," are able to live their everyday lives. Lives of inexorable tedium punctuated, particularly toward the end, by incredible anguish. I must confess, I have come to love you humans to the point, at least in God's eyes, of corruption. And unfortunately, God will allow my limited intervention in only one human life, Jamey Maxwell's. I wish this was not the case for there is another in this story that I have come to especially love. Luis Moya. I will tell you why in just a while.

Jamey Maxwell arrives at the Torres County courthouse in Sandersville. The limestone courthouse is an optical illusion in that it looks much larger than it actually is. One reason is that the backdrop to the courthouse, a limestone hill covered with greasewood and mesquite shrubs which, because of perspective, appear to be large trees in the distance, therefore by rote extrapolation of human consciousness renders a skewed image of the relatively small public building. The other reason is that most people's minds will not let them accept a county courthouse being this small. But it has a certain elegant simplicity, which speaks of a much earlier time when embellishments, as seen in more recently built courthouses, were considered frivolous and pointless. A solid, two-story building of white limestone blocks, in what some might call Territorial style.

The population of Torres County is 3,873 folks, predominately Hispanic. It is a vast, empty county in a vast, empty universe. It has only three law enforcement officers: Sheriff Lon Hayes, Deputy Morgan Davis (semi-fondly known hereabouts as "Barney Fife") and Deputy Luis Moya, whom I love dearly. As much as a Watcher can love a human.

Here is why I love Luis Moya: he is defective. At least to other humans. His defect is his shortness. Yes,

school. Luis, although well liked by all of his classmates, never found the courage to ask Victoria Hernández, or any other girl, out. He knew he was short. Deficient. But now the prom was approaching and the pressure was on Luis Moya to find a date. A common human ritual which must be observed. His friends and family began asking in January whom Luis was asking to the prom in April. And friends and family began filling Luis' head with optimistic thoughts about how many girls "would love to go to the prom" with him. Eventually, out of a combination of fatigue, false hope, and desperation, Luis decided he would do it. He would ask Victoria Hernández, e*l amor de su vida,* to go the prom with him. He had checked with friends to make sure she had not already been asked by another.

That morning, the morning which he would take the biggest leap of his life, he vomited in the bathroom at home. Then he went to school. Between third and forth periods, he approached Vicki at her locker. And as teenage girls usually are, she was surrounded by a few of her friends. Luis, sick, nervous, excited, tapped Vicki lightly on her shoulder. When she turned around, he looked in her eyes (which meant he had to look up, since Vicki, by now, was five feet six inches tall.) For a moment, the words would not come out, and he looked down. But Luis, who even at this young age possessed courage and dignity, raised his head and said, "I was wondering if you would go to the prom with me?"

First, there was silence, then Vicki's girlfriends began covering their mouths in a very weak attempt to hide their snickering. Vicki looked down at Luis, and said, "I don't think so." She turned to her girlfriends and they all, simultaneously, broke into cruel laughter. That laughter still rings in Luis Moya's ears.

Luis Moya is not married and he will never be. He can never again in this life risk the humiliation and the crushing blow of rejection by a woman. Any woman. He has dedicated his life to his job as a law enforcement officer. It is both his refuge and his reason for living.

Now, let me tell you about the investigation. After Manuelito discovered the bodies of Billy and Kristin Garnett, he hurried home to his grandfather, Diego Castillo. Diego Castillo, who did not have a telephone in his home, then walked a quarter of a mile to the house of the ranch foreman, Vicente Arrisola. Vicente Arrisola then called the Sheriff's Office in Sandersville and spoke to Deputy Morgan Davis, aka "Barney Fife." The conversation went something like this.

"Sir, I would like to report two bodies found on the Galvan Ranch," said Mr. Arrisola.

"Well, are they dead or alive?" asked Deputy Davis.

"Sir, they are both dead," said Mr. Arrisola.

"How do you know they're dead?" asked Deputy Davis.

"Well, sir, I think most of their heads are missing," answered Mr. Arrisola.

"Oh," responded Deputy Davis.

"Can you send someone right away?" asked Mr. Arrisola.

"Well, now, Sheriff Hayes is out looking for a couple of stray cows and Deputy Moya is home at lunch, so we can't come right away. Can you go back and secure the bodies until we get there?"

Vicente Arrisola was beginning to regret ever making this phone call, but answered, "Well, I guess so, but please try to hurry."

"We'll do our best," responded Deputy Davis.

"Would you like directions to the bodies?" asked Mr. Arrisola.

"That would be great," answered Deputy Davis.

Three hours later, the Three Stooges showed up at the murder scene. Texas Ranger Earl McVay arrived an hour later. By then, most of the damage had been done, thanks, primarily, to Deputy Morgan Davis. His footprints and fingerprints would be found on an amazing amount, in fact on the vast majority of evidence. And in such a short time. This despite the fact that Luis Moya, upon their arrival, had whispered diplomatically to Sheriff Hayes that maybe Deputy Davis would be of more help if he returned to the office and answered phone calls. Sheriff Lon Hayes was not accustomed to making such important decisions hastily, so by the time he decided Deputy Moya had made a good suggestion, Deputy Davis had pretty well fucked up the entire crime scene. Ranger McVay was not nearly as diplomatic as Deputy Moya and after arriving and surveying the situation told Deputy Davis to "get the fuck" off the Galvan Ranch and "never, ever, come back."

Sheriff Hayes, relieved the tirade was directed at anyone but him, graciously and thankfully capitulated the crime scene to Earl McVay and slinked away to the main gate of the Galvan Ranch to "secure the perimeter." Ranger McVay asked Luis Moya to assist him in taking photographs, making measurements and drawings of the crime scene, and tagging and bagging what little untainted evidence remained. McVay had met Moya a few years earlier on a missing persons case and was immediately impressed with him, despite his stature. The missing person case turned out to be a case of a sixteen-year-old female running off with her twenty-two-year-old boyfriend. She returned to Sandersville after a week of living the life of the homeless.

The evidence was gathered and the justice of the peace finally arrived to pronounce the two victims legally dead. Ranger McVay asked Sheriff Hayes to stay with the bodies until the nearest medical examiner, in this case located in Midland, could arrive to transport the bodies for autopsy. The victims, a male and a female, had no wallet, no purse, no forms of identification, no distinguishing marks, no scars, no tattoos. Fingerprints might be helpful if the victims had criminal backgrounds, military backgrounds, or worked for a government agency which may have required fingerprinting. McVay doubted he would be so lucky. His pessimism was based on the way the couple was dressed and his gut feeling. The bodies had obviously been there for several days judging by the state of decomposition. Also, the wounds, undoubtedly instantly fatal, were horrendous. McVay believed it would take dental records to make positive identification of the victims.

McVay asked the Sheriff if he could borrow Deputy Moya to help interview the witnesses, particularly Manuelito Castillo. Hayes, of course, obliged and was thankful McVay didn't ask the Sheriff to accompany him. Sheriff Hayes' enthusiasm for his job was waning rapidly, the excitement of handling a murder case a distant sensation after just three hours. He had gained a new appreciation for chasing stray livestock.

Vicente Arrisola accompanied McVay and Moya to the Castillo adobe hovel. Manuelito was there, as was his grandfather. Manuelito was still in a state of shock and was not much help with details. The only real detail he could provide was the sight of *muchos alacranes del diablo*, which he repeated over and over. Although Ranger McVay spoke decent Spanish, Deputy Moya had to translate *alacranes del diablo* for him. Since Ranger McVay had never seen a whipscorpion, he wasn't sure exactly what Manuelito was talking about. McVay assumed Manuelito was speaking in hyperbole. Deputy Moya knew better. He sensed there was great importance to the *alacranes* which Manuelito described, but kept this hunch to himself. Later, he would find someone to share this hunch with: Jamey Maxwell.

Jamey walks into the small courthouse and finds the Sheriff's Office. It doesn't take long. Luis Moya is the only person in the sparse headquarters. When Jamey Maxwell introduces himself to Luis Moya there is an instant connection. You know why. It's their respective imperfections. And their innate, and possibly inane, kindness. They are two misshapen peas in a misshapen pod.

After several hours of enjoying each others' company, first at the courthouse, then over coffee at Lupe's, Luis takes Jamey Maxwell to the Galvan Ranch — to the murder scene. When Jamey steps out of the Torres County's beat-up Ford Taurus, he hears a faint voice inside his head. He can barely make out the words, but he knows they are not in English. They sound something like, "*Aalah okhasiah, Aalah okhasiah, Aalah okhasiah.*" Of course, this is Aramaic. It means "God is holy, God is holy, blah, blah, blah." It's the Cheribum. They say that a lot.

Luis tells Jamey where the bodies were found. Luis tells him about the investigation and the theories bandied back and forth, mostly between Luis and Ranger McVay. Since Luis wanted to remain in the realm of reality, Sheriff Hayes' and Deputy Davis' theories were not discussed. Most significant to Luis and Jamey was the statement taken from Manuelito Castillo, the sheepherder. Both Luis and Jamey know, without a iota of doubt (or "iola of doubt," as St. Charles, Jamey's dad, used to say) that the most important evidence in this case was the presence of *los alacranes del diablo* — the vinegaroons. They do not need to tell each other this; it has been communicated both telepathically and empathetically. Luis wants to show Jamey a magical place, a place where Luis' grandfather, a full-blooded Kickapoo, took the grandkids when they were children.

Can I digress for a moment? Can we talk about life? Human life? How much human life really sucks? It makes me wonder why I like humans so much. It's a mystery, wrapped in an enigma, inside a riddle, then stuffed up your ass like a giant suppository — with serrated edges. Maybe it's because you haven't committed the unforgivable sin, at least unforgivable to us

Watchers, of being boring. Speaking of asses and suppositories, your God; the One you occasionally get down on your knees to worship; gave you humans large intestines, small intestines, rectums; which I like to call assholes; with which to dispose of your feces. Your shit. Does that sound right to you? Does that sound like the Guy that created this beautiful, unfathomable universe, not to mention Heaven, and Hell. Don't you think He could have done a little better than that? Assholes and shit? Makes you wonder if maybe He should have rested on the sixth day. Or the fifth. With this in mind, do you really think you are created in His image? Thank God…Thank God…I am an angel.

And when I ask if I can digress, I mean really digress.

Life in the Stone Age was a bitch. Then it was over, soon. Cro-Magnons seldom lived past the age of twenty. And that was the men. Life was really harsh for the women who basically had little or no value in the grand scheme of things. Even pussy wasn't worth that much back then. Thus, was the shitty life of the Cro-Magnon. I could have told you that. I was there.

Before that, the life span for what you now call the Australopithecus was even shorter and shittier. Most died in their teens. Lots of widows, orphans, etc. And, remember, God was around then. So, what do you folks think of this? Not much, probably. Doesn't really pertain to you, does it? Or does it?

Oh, and Neanderthals came along between the Australopithecus and the Cro-Magnon. Guess what? Their lives really sucked big green slimy ones, too. I'm talking a complete fucking bummer. I could have told you that. I was there. And, here's the sad, or maybe not, part: unlike you fucking know-it-all humans of today, they did not have a clue whom to blame for their misery. They had vague ideas of demons and gods, but had a hard time finding the time to ponder such things when they were starving to death or when a fucking saber-toothed tiger was trying to eat their collective ass. Not much time to play the "blame game" with that going on. Had they had just a little free time, they may have figured out at Whom to point the finger.

So, here's the deal. Somewhere between ancient man and now, humans came to believe they have a purpose. Not sure where that came from. Not from God. He forgot to give you a purpose, other than relief from His ennui of being. So for millennia, with a few exceptions, people were born, they struggled to survive, then they died. Along the way something happened. Maybe it was two thousand years ago or maybe centuries earlier. You developed a sense that your lives had meaning. Trust me when I tell you this: you were, and still are, wrong. The unfortunate result is your artificially inherent desire to live longer. And you keep finding new and creative ways to prolong the misery. As recently as 1900, human life expectancy was only 49 years. You live too long now. You keep coming up with new reasons to exist. Stop it.

Chapter 4

That Old Time Religion

Deputy Luis Moya and Jamey Maxwell, the two defective detectives, arrive at Seminole Canyon State Park. Luis has something to show Jamey. They will hike into Seminole Canyon to a cave, one that is off limits to tourists, but not to a man with a badge. Luis meets with the park superintendent, briefly explains the need for visiting the cave, leaving out all of the important details. Luis and Jamey begin the mile and a half hike, down the steep and narrow canyon. The scenery is magnificent in its majestic harshness. The reddish-brown cliffs, three hundred feet high in places, provide sanctuary to nesting raptors. The wind and water-worn formations are proof of man's insignificance on this earth. Jamey sees it as a specific reminder from God of this fact. Not since he was nine years old has Jamey Maxwell ever believed any differently, so to him God is just being redundant, as usual.

If one could see this part of West Texas from the air, as I can, one would see some very interesting rock formations, which could make one believe a race of giants actually existed here eons ago. On either side of the

Devils River (it was not called that back then...guess that was before the Devil made it to West Texas) white and beige limestone is laid out in a striated pattern resembling muscle tissue on a colossal scale. More specifically, muscle tissue found on the human torso. And these formations go on for miles and miles. So, with just a little imagination (we Seraphs have more than a little) one can picture a vast battlefield in which tens of thousands of enormous warriors fell. And let's just say, that in some sort of bizarre ritual by the victors, each enemy warrior was skinned. And let's just say in most cases, while still alive. And let's just say they were then turned on their stomachs, leaving only rippling muscle tissue of their backs, buttocks, and legs exposed to the virulent desert sun. After millennia of dessication, the tissue has petrified, leaving only the limestone facsimile. And from the air, the greasewood scrub, the sotol and lechuguilla, growing between the undulating striations, resemble forms of mold and fungus which might have grown upon the rotting flesh and then persisted for time upon time. But again, it's probably just my imagination.

Luis and Jamey finally reach Paint Cave. Paint Cave is impressive in many ways, not the least being the large opening under a protruding boulder. Large enough for fourteen men to ride into on horseback at one time. An event repeated many times during the nineteenth century by outlaws, U.S. cavalry troops, Apache and Comanche warriors. But long before that, aboriginal people painted wild animals on the walls. Buffalo, puma, white-tailed deer, pronghorn antelopes...and vinegaroons. This is what Luis Moya brought Jamey Maxwell to see.

Luis is talking to Jamey, but Jamey is not listening. There has been an explosion — inside his head. And the resulting shrapnel is as beautiful as it is horrifying. A glimpse of the past or maybe a quick look into the future. It is not Earth. It might be Heaven. In fact, it is Heaven. I have decided to bestow this gift upon Jamey Maxwell, much as God did upon Enoch, once upon a time. You ask what purpose this may serve? Will this help Jamey on his quest to find the bad guys? I doubt it. But every once in a while we angels, we "sons of God," we *bene elohim,* just want to have fun. So sue me.

And now for my amusement and Jamey Maxwell's useless, but further, enlightenment:

Behold, in the vision, clouds invite him and a mist summons him, and the course of the stars and lightnings speed and hasten him. And he draws nigh to a wall which is built of crystals and surrounded by tongues of fire, and it begins to affright him. And he goes into the tongues of fire and draws nigh to a large house which is built of crystals. And the walls of the house are like a tesselated floor made of crystals, and its groundwork is of crystal. Its ceilings are like the path of the stars and the lightnings, and between them are fiery Cherubim, and their heaven is as clear as water. A flaming fire surrounds the walls, and its portals blaze with fire. And he enters into that house, and it is hot as fire and cold as ice. There are no delights of life therein. Fear covers him, and trembling grabs hold of him. And as he quakes and trembles, he falls upon his face. And he beholds a vision, and lo! there is a second house, greater than the first, and the entire portal stands open before him, and it is built of flames of fire. And in every respect it so excels in splendor and magnificence and extent that he cannot describe to you its splendor and its extent. And its floor is of fire, and above it is lightnings and the path of the stars, and its ceiling also is flaming fire. And he looks and sees therein a lofty throne. Its appearance is as crystal, and the wheel thereof as the shining sun, and there is the vision of Cherubim. And from underneath the throne come streams of flaming fire so that he can not look thereon. And the Great Glory sits thereon, and His raiment shines more brightly than the sun and is whiter than any snow. None of the angels can enter or behold His face by reason of the magnificence and glory and no flesh could behold Him. The flaming fire is round about Him, and a great fire stands before Him, and none around can draw nigh Him. Ten thousand times ten thousand stand before Him, yet He needs no counselor. And the most holy ones who are nigh to Him did not leave by night nor depart from Him. And until now Jamey Maxwell has been prostrate on his face, trembling. And the Lord calls to him with His own mouth, and says to him: "Come hither, Jamey Maxwell, and hear my word." And one of the holy ones comes to him and wakes him, and He makes him rise up and approach the door. And Jamey Maxwell bows his face downwards.

Okay, okay, this scene is pretty much straight from The Book of Enoch, but no one ever accused us Seraphs of being original. Besides, it's a scene I like very much, although, I personally have never seen anything like it. I just wanted to impress my client. I think I did.

"Mr. Maxwell, Mr. Maxwell! Are you okay?" Luis Moya is worried. Something seems terribly wrong with his new friend.

Jamey finally snaps to. "Sorry, yes. I'm fine. Just a little headache. I'm okay. This is a very interesting place." He is looking around the cave and, despite its size, it feels confining; claustrophobic.

"This is what I was telling you about," Luis says pointing to the left back wall of the cave.

The indirect sunlight, and Luis' flashlight, illuminate the petroglyphs. There are the bison, the wildcats, and finally, the flashlight and Jamey's eyes find the vinegaroons. The drawings show a prone body covered with the creatures. The crude illustrations seem to indicate a spray coming from the tails directed toward the victim's face. He or she appears to be unconscious or dead. Wavy lines are drawn as if something is hovering above the body.

That claustrophobic feeling has now become unbearable and Jamey tells Luis he needs some fresh air. He turns and walks rapidly out of the cave into the unrestrained West Texas sunlight. He tells Luis he needs to go to the Sandersville Library and look up some things on the Internet. Then he grins and asks, "Does Sandersville have a library? If so, does it have Internet?" Luis smiles and nods his head.

On their way back to Sandersville, Jamey turns to Luis and asks, "Have you ever heard of The Book of Enoch?" Luis replies that he has not. Jamey then asks, "Does the word 'nefilim' or 'nefalim' mean anything to you? Maybe in Spanish?" Again, Luis replies in the negative.

Then Luis asks, "What is The Book of Enoch about?"

Jamey replies, "I don't really know. Something to do with the Bible. Enoch was an ancient prophet, I think. I don't even know where I've heard about it. But I think the word 'nefalim' or 'nefilim' is in the book. That's what I want to check on the Internet."

Luis takes Jamey to the Sandersville library and they spend the rest of the day discovering *mucha* info about The Book of Enoch, the Nephilim…and vinegaroons. Afterwards, enlightenment seems further away for both of them. The Book of Enoch is confusing, contradictory, possibly sacrilegious, at least in Luis' mind. Both agree that Nephilim are mythical creatures that could not possibly have existed.

Oh, the human mind. Even at its most curious and unprejudiced, it is still so fucking inadequate. I try and I try to elucidate. Jamey Maxwell, my unwary minion, is a hard nut to crack. But crack him, I will.

Jamey and Luis discuss their findings over supper at Chuy's, the best of four small Mexican restaurants in Sandersville. And, not coincidentally, the workplace of a certain Victoria Coronado, formerly Victoria Hernández. Before she finished high school, Vicki Hernández became pregnant and married the star running back of the Sandersville Javelinas football team, Benjamín Coronado. Things were wonderful for almost an entire month, at which time Ben woke up one morning and realized he was married. Long story short: divorce. Vicki, seeking other male authority figures in her life, began sleeping around; is now an unmarried mother of four children. And, now she believes she is in love with Luis Moya. Oops. Too late.

Funny thing is, Luis keeps coming back to Chuy's on a daily basis. What does this say about the state of affairs of human beings? Diddly-squat. Diddly-fucking-squat.

Jamey keeps returning to the thing that intrigued him the most about their research: that the Great Flood, which Noah and his family survived, was God's attempt to wipe out the Nephilim. To be safe, he wiped out virtually all human and animal life too. Now, that is one angry, or scared, God. It is even in the Bible: Genesis, Chapter 6. How many people in the world, how many Christians, are even aware of this? Not many, he and Luis agreed.

Jamey asks Luis to take him to the Galván Ranch to speak with Manuelito. He wants to ask the young shepherd about the vinegaroons. For reasons he cannot explain, Jamey Maxwell needs to see the expression on Manuelito's face. Once again Luis finds himself in the Castillo adobe abode, speaking briefly with Manuelito's grandfather in Spanish. Then with Manuelito. Through Luis, Jamey asks basically the same questions presented by Ranger McVay. No new information is imparted, Earl McVay having done a very thorough job, as Texas Rangers invariably do.

Jamey now tells Luis Moya to ask Manuelito to describe the *alacranes del diablo*. The vinegaroons. The sweet young shepherd's eyes instantly flash the fear of gods and devils, angels and demons. The young man cannot speak. There is no need for him to. Subliminal information on a cosmic scale is now imparted, beyond the jurisdiction of the Texas Rangers. Jamey Maxwell soaks it up on a cellular level.

As they are leaving the Castillo place, Jamey says to

Luis, "Will you ask the old man what the floor is made of here?" Jamey is taken by the patina of the beautiful brown floor, the texture, even the earthy smell, which for a moment makes the humble mud home seem like a palace. Luis asks Manuelito's grandfather. The grandfather answers, "*Mierda de vaca,*" and smiles. Manuelito smiles. Luis Moya turns to Jamey Maxwell, smiles, and says, "Cow shit. The floor is made of cow shit." Jamey Maxwell smiles. Then all four men's smiles turn to laughter.

To find out more about vinegaroons, Jamey plans on heading to Alpine in the morning to visit a certain professor at Sul Ross State University. He is going to visit Dr. Bing Goodall, the foremost expert on vinegaroons in the state of Texas, at least according to the good ol' Internet. The Internet has become a very useful device with which to communicate with my little buddy, Jamey Maxwell.

He is in another motel room. This time in Marathon, Texas. The name says it all. Sleep finds Jamey Maxwell *una vez más*.

The dreams are still coming. This time Jamey is sitting at the little kitchen table at St. Charles Place with his dad, St. Charles. And his wife Connie. They are young again. Charles says, "I bet you think I'm happy in Heaven now. Living the "Life of Reilly." It ain't like that though. It ain't like that at all." Jamey's beloved father smiles and shows a set of rotting green teeth. He says, "Because of you I got sent to Hell. Proud of yourself?"

El vejarrón sin piernas, the old fart without legs, somehow manages to interject himself into Jamey

Maxwell's dream. He tells Jamey, "Look son, this is not real. Look at me. Listen to me. Your father is at peace now. Let it go. You don't have time for this. Things are happening all around you. Wake up and smell the shit."

I hate that no-legged-grizzled-cocksucking-do-gooding-motherfucker. Don't bother pardoning my French.

Chapter 5

Bugs and Those That Love Them

Sul Ross State University, named after a former governor of Texas, sits on a rise at the eastern edge of Alpine in West Texas. God's country. Does that make Sul Ross State God's university? Maybe. Alpine, population 6,319, is the epicenter of the West Texas ranching industry. Ruminants such as sheep, goats, cattle, pronghorn antelopes, and mule deer subsist on the scrub grasses covering the slopes of the hills, some of which swell into actual mountains. Sul Ross State University, a ranching college through and through, chose as its mascot the Lobo, dreaded enemy of all ruminants. Obviously irony abounds in West Texas.

This seemingly provincial college of some 2,000 students has as an adjunct faculty member a quiet, unassuming professor of entomology, Bing Goodall. Dr. Goodall is affectionately known as "Squeaky" by all 2,000 students, 161 faculty members, 233 support staff, and most of the 6,319 residents of Alpine. He doesn't know that is his nickname. This is because he spends most of his time alone, studying bugs, usually not tuned into frequencies upon which human voices are

are transmitted. It's not that Dr. Goodall — Squeaky — is anti-social. He just prefers not to socialize with the species *homo erectus*. And speaking of frequencies which transmit human voices, when Dr. Goodall talks he sounds like your Donald Duck — on helium. Hence, the nickname.

Dr. Goodall has never been married. He's never been seen in the company of a woman. In fact, the joke around campus is this: If you ever run across a cockroach with a human head, don't stomp on it, it's just Squeaky Junior. Oh, your college students, the perennial purveyors of perverse preposterousness.

"Ah yes, vinegaroons. Whipscorpions. Scientific name of the local species: *Mastigoproctus giganteus*. But much more colorfully referred to as "mule killers" here in West Texas," Dr. Goodall explains. Jamey Maxwell is standing in Dr. Goodall's office, but he might as well not be. All Jamey had to do was ask the question and Dr. Goodall was immediately thrust into his unilateral and exquisitely lonely world of creepy-crawlys.

"Vinegaroons are, personally, my favorite of the arachnids," Dr. Goodall continues in his Donald Duck-on-steroids voice. "Whipscorpions, order *Uropygi*, bear some resemblance to scorpions, but differ in the form of their pedipalps. Much shorter and stouter. Also different, their antenna-like first legs and their whip-bearing abdomen. The aforementioned *Mastigoproctus giganteus* can reach 6.5 centimeters in length, and ranges throughout the southern part of the United States. Whipscorpions are nocturnal, spending the day under rocks, in burrows, and other protected places. They feed on other arthropods, slugs, and worms.

Their prey is seized and torn with the pedipalps before it is eaten. Mating is indirect and involves the deposition of a spermatophore by the male. A strange courtship dance is performed, similar to that of other scorpions. But while dancing, the male holds the female's long sensory legs, rather than her pedipalps. Quite sensuous, in my opinion. When it is time for egg-laying, the female secludes herself in a retreat and lays from seven to thirty-five eggs. She remains in the shelter with the eggs until they have hatched and the young have undergone several molts. After the young have dispersed, she dies. Kind of sad, in a way."

Jamey Maxwell wants to beam Dr. Goodall back to Earth, so he asks, "Have you ever heard of a group, say hundreds, of vinegaroons attacking a human?"

Dr. Goodall looks quizzically at Jamey, as if he just appeared out of thin air, but doesn't speak.

"Are you okay?" Jamey asks.

Dr. Goodall frowns and responds. "That is a very strange question."

Jamey says nothing.

"Mr. Maxwell, my family grew up in this area. Most people think I am from another state, another country, or perhaps, another planet. I am aware of what people say about me; what they think about me. I am different from most people and I have always been. I enjoy being different.

"But my family, for the most part, is *puro* West Texas. My great grandfather, who was raised in Tennessee, came to West Texas in 1882 to work on the railroad. He died in Sandersville three days short of his ninety-third birthday. It was 1957. When he was dying, he told me a story. I was nine years old at the time. I didn't know he was dying. I knew he was old, but being nine years old, I thought everyone you loved lived forever. I thought only people you didn't know died.

"My great grandfather's story went something like this: Southern Pacific was working on tunnel number two on the west side of the Pecos River, between Eagle Nest, which is present day Langtry, and Seminole Canyon. A tent city of about two thousand people bloomed on the rocky hill just above the tunnel. The workers named it Vinegaroon because of the strange scorpion-like creature which was ubiquitous. It was ubiquitous because the workers' job was to move rocks around. Had they not been moving rocks, they may never have seen a vinegaroon. What they would see under the rocks was a solitary whipscorpion. With one notable exception. On the evening of June 15, an Italian working on the tunnel ventured down to the Rio Grande River and was struck by lightning. Even to unsuperstitious people, of which there were few in Vinegaroon at that time, this would have been an ominous sign. A small cemetery had become a necessity for the little tent city and when they went to bury the unfortunate Italian the next morning a strange and horrific thing happened. When my great grandfather told me this part, for an instant he looked younger than me. He actually began to curl up in his bed. By the time he finished the story he was in a fetal position. The thought of my great grandfather being afraid was a concept I had never considered. Of course, he was old when I was born and his valiant days were behind him. But we were very close and he told me many tales which led me to believe he was incredibly heroic. He and my father were the bravest people in the world as far as I was concerned. But seeing him afraid made me afraid. That fear has stuck to me and probably caused me to become what I am today. You see, I went into entomology and arachnology to prove what my great grandfather told me could not possibly be true. I have studied the whipscorpion, *Mastigoproctus giganteus*, for thirty years to prove my great grandfather's deathbed story was delusional. Or that if it did happen, it had to be some sort of mass fantasy — a St. Vitus' Dance without the dance. That all the men who saw it were mistaken. That all the men who saw it were actually seeing some sort of phantom image. And now you come to me with your question and now the fear of a nine-year-old child is as fresh as yesterday.

"Mr. Maxwell, what my great grandfather told me was this: when they put the Italian in the shallow rock grave, within seconds he was covered with hundreds, maybe thousands of vinegaroons. And they were very angry. And they were looking for something. It made my great grandfather afraid to die."

Jamey Maxwell remains silent.

Dr. Goodall leans forward in his swivel chair and with a solemn voice asks, "Now, why are you here, Mr. Maxwell. Are you here to make me afraid to die?"

Jamey Maxwell replies, "Maybe we all should be afraid to die. But fortunately or unfortunately, depending on how you look at, most of us are too afraid to live to worry about dying."

Dr. Goodall's squeaky voice drops an octave and he says, "That's why I like the invertebrate world so much

— they don't think. What an incredible blessing God bestowed upon them."

"Your great grandfather said the vinegaroons were looking for something. Did he say what he thought they were looking for?" Jamey asks.

"He didn't have to say. What else could they have been looking for…except for a soul?" Dr. Goodall replies.

Jamey Maxwell is in a motel room in Del Rio. He is asleep.

He is dreaming again. He does that a lot now. Miguel and Daniel are talking to him. They are at Zenia's Place, sitting at Jamey's old favorite table. Even in the dream, Jamey knows this is strange. Miguel never goes to bars. Neither does Daniel, since Angelita's death.

Miguel says, "*Mi amigo*, give it a rest. This is not your business. *No es tu trabajo*. Come home. Stay with me and Daniel. Be *estúpido* like us. Let the world take care of itself. It does not matter. *No le hace*."

Then Daniel says, "Yes, Jamey, come home. We need you."

When Jamey Maxwell hears this, he awakes. Even in a dream, he knows this is wrong. Daniel does not talk like this. Jamey feels like he is being manipulated. He is. Aren't we all?

Chapter 6

Enlightenment

There are things I haven't told you yet. I guess I wanted you to get to know me better before you begin to judge me. And, God knows, how judgmental you humans can be. I, like most Watchers, am very insecure. For good reason. God does not trust us. For good reason. Watchers are notoriously corrupt and have been since the beginning of time. We tend to covet. Specifically, we tend to covet what mankind has. Azazel was the first to cross that line back when man was new or should I say when woman was new. Azazel lusted after the first women. He was mesmerized by them, although he had no clue what they were about. Sounds like most men of today, right ladies? And in case you're wondering, we Seraphs or Watchers, can be whatever sex we choose to be; which, as we like to joke, doubles our chances for a date on a Saturday night. Azazel held sway and convinced two hundred other Watchers to descend to Earth and cavort with women. No, I was not one of them. They were led by Samlazaz, Araklba, Rameel, Sariel, and, of course, their leader, Azazel. This cavorting led to abominable offspring, the Nephilim. Bastards and Reprobates — Children of Fornication — that's how God refers to them. Your Bible refers to them as "the mighty men that were of old, the men of renown." This reference is so…inadequate…deceptive…vague.

Enoch and other Hebrew prophets describe them as terrible giants, but they weren't giants. They were, however, terrible, at least in God's eyes. And when it gets right down to it, that's all that counts, isn't it?

What the Nephilim were, and still are, are creatures without souls. These creatures look and act just like any other human beings. They are human beings, for that matter. And on the face of it, they are neither good nor bad. They don't know they are soulless. As a matter of fact, many historical figures, some of them beloved, were Nephilim. But they are soulless human beings and for that God has decreed they must all be destroyed. Since Watchers are the ones that created the Nephilim, God does not trust them, or should I say us, to participate in the destruction. That is where a few special humans, such as Jamey Maxwell, come in. They were put here on this earth exclusively for that task. It's kind of sad really.

What most people do not realize, what Jamey Maxwell and Luis Moya now know, is this: God precipitated the Great Flood, which made Noah famous, not to destroy mankind, but to destroy the Nephilim. In the ancient days, God feared they would corrupt the bloodline of the coming Messiah. The Nephilim during the time of Noah were running rampant. Kind of like cockroaches. So God tried to exterminate them all at once. Unfortunately, one of them, the wife of Japheth, made it onto the Ark, so their bloodline persisted and does until this very day.

Angels are also notorious liars. Believe me. Ha ha! Or as your TV character, Archie Bunker, would say, "It's in the Bible, look it up!" We lie because we covet. We covet what humans have and we covet God's love. And since God loves humans more than us, we lie and covet even more. Even though we also love humans. Having to compete against humans for God's love and against God for humans' love makes us a rather pathetic species, I suppose. And now that I've told you this, I have no more reason to lie to you. Especially regarding the matter at hand.

As Jamey Maxwell drives Daniel and Taz through town in his old blue S-10, he becomes conscious of something about Dos Cruces to which he has been previously oblivious. The secret has been here for years, waiting to be discovered. Or rather exposed. He feels the fool for not recognizing it until now. But he shouldn't be too hard on himself. Jamey Maxwell has had many reasons to be self-absorbed — unobservant — for the past few years. As the trio drives past Zenia's Place, the Texas Cafe, Reynaldos (oh, how Jamey misses Angelita), and two other drinking establishments which have no name but "Bar," the quiet cries out to Jamey Maxwell. Having grown up in South Texas, Jamey knows there is a fundamental element found in communities with Hispanic populations which is missing in Dos Cruces. That element is joy. It is usually manifested in song and dance; *corridos, comparsas, boleros, mariachis*; in bars, cafes, and homes. There is no singing and dancing in Dos Cruces. There has been neither for the four years that Jamey Maxwell has subsisted here and he is quite sure that it stopped on a specific day many years ago. Say June 24, 1965.

I have subliminally imparted this information to Jamey. On that day, the joy was extracted from Dos Cruces. Sucked out by the Cosmic Vacuum Cleaner. And Jamey is also quite sure that it went unnoticed by everyone in the community. Joy ceased to exist that day in Dos Cruces. God decreed that joy be abolished and no one took notice. No one objected. The guilty, that is to say pretty much the entire population of Dos Cruces, unconsciously accepted the sentence and were intuitively thankful it was not more severe. No one spoke of it then and no one speaks of it now. This sentence was handed down on that day and will be carried out in perpetuity upon this forsaken town. There is one, and only one, exception. That exception is riding in the truck with Jamey Maxwell: Daniel Galvan, the goatboy.

Let me tell you a little about Miguel Veras' wife. Her name was Graciela. She married Miguel in 1939. She was fourteen; he was seventeen. She was a beautiful child bride. But before she was a child bride, she was a prostitute in *la zona roja*, the red light district, in Nuevo Laredo. It was during the Great Depression, and, yes, the humans of Mexico suffered as much or more than the humans of the United States, particularly in the border towns. The difference being most people in Mexico have always lived in a great depression. Graciela was trying to survive. As many young women have done throughout history when they have nothing else to sell, they sell their bodies. And often their souls (but, not in the case of Graciela Rincon). Miguel was a young street vendor when he first met Graciela. He did not know she was a prostitute. He did know she was beautiful. He called her *linda paloma.* Pretty dove. As she grew older, people around her came to believe she was a *bruja.* A witch. Why, you ask? Well, because of a genetic defect, or a genetic miracle, depending on one's point of view. You see, Graciela had extremely high levels of HDL (good cholesterol) as well as unusual levels of HGH (human growth hormone) and lastly, the practically perfect ratio of estrogen to testosterone. And what did this all mean? It meant Graciela was virtually ageless. She became more beautiful as she grew older. Before she died at the age of thirty-nine, she was often mistaken for a teenage girl. People, mostly women, concluded she must be a witch. Oh, human jealousy. It is such a motherfucker.

Here's a little inside information — a scoop — for you folks. On June 24, 1965, Miguel's wife, Graciela, was raped and murdered by a group of men in Dos Cruces. The leader of this wretched gang, Arturo Castro, was a relative newcomer to town. All the other men had spent their entire pointless lives in Dos Cruces. These men were looking for something to relieve their endless boredom and Arturo Castro accommodated with this amusing aspiration. These men, except for Arturo, had no intention of committing murder. But Arturo convinced them, and rightly so, that they really had no other choice. After spending an entire afternoon raping Graciela, what else could they do? Miguel had been out of town that day, visiting his sister in Nuevo Laredo. She was dying. As was, it turns out, his beautiful wife.

As for the wives of these accidental murderers, they knew about it. They knew their husbands had at least witnessed the rape and killing of what they considered to be *una* unGodly beautiful *bruja*. But because of the *machismo* culture these women were born into, none of them came forward and the crime went unsolved. In reality, the white law enforcement officials in charge of Losoya County were none too concerned about a Mexican — a former prostitute — being murdered in Dos Cruces. The case was closed shortly after it was opened with this notation in the file. Cause of death "unknown." There. Aren't you glad I told you?

Jamey begins a memory backtrack, considering all of the people he has encountered since moving to Dos Cruces. The late, sweet Marisol; the late, sweet Angelita; her grandmother Dora; Ramon Falcón; Violet's crazy sister; Daniel's family; Miguel Vera; all the others. No joy to be found. Barely even the illusion of joy. They didn't even know how to fake it.

Jamey had intended to stop in and buy Daniel supper at Reynaldo's, but instead turns the S-10 around and heads back to Miguel's workshop. As they cross the railroad track, Jamey sees another *hombre retardado*, the "train director," waiting for the Southern Pacific train to come by. He is thirty-five years old chronologically. His left leg is grotesquely deformed and he drags it around like a separate entity. It serves only as a balance mechanism for when he throws the rocks. His velocity and accuracy are very impressive. The train director has an uncanny internal clock synchronized with the comings and goings of trains through Dos Cruces. The trains never stop here. The train director throws rocks at the trains as they pass. It's his job. He's very good at it. But he finds no joy in it.

Jamey drops Daniel off at the workshop and heads to his humble abode, St. Charles Place. He calls Janette Dean and says, "I need to see you."

She asks, "Professionally or personally?"

Jamey replies, "Both. Neither. I don't know."

She says, "Come on up. I'll meet you at our usual place. Can you be here at two thirty? A warning though, I'm bringing you home with me. We both need to talk." Jamey tries to speak, but cannot. "I'll see you then," Janette says and hangs up.

Jamey Maxwell finds himself at the home of Dr. Janette Dean. He is surveying the surroundings which look all too familiar to him. He could easily be in his old home. The one where Connie Lee, Julie, Josie, and hope once resided. All of them are gone now. Dr. Dean obviously has the same decorating gene as his Connie Lee. It's that gene that God bestows upon attractive, middle-class women. Jamey is overcome with grief. There is also a more ominous aura residing here. Jamey, once again chooses to ignore.

Janette, dressed in baggy jeans and maternity t-shirt, has that radiant look most pregnant women exhibit. It appears superficial somehow. She looks into Jamey's eyes. He feels her piercing his cornea, hitting the retina, traveling up the optic nerve, splintering at the optic chiasma, finding her way into parts of his brain that should have died five years ago. Janette is trying, in desperation, to tell him something; but the message is not getting through. And, the saddest part is, Janette Dean is trying to transmit a message of which she is not even aware; regarding an event that is imminent, inevitable, and yet still unknown to her. God could tell her, and Jamey Maxwell, if He chose to. But He will not. I know Him. To God, the message is overwhelmingly tragic; but ultimately distracting. It will serve no useful purpose.

Instead, Jamey begins to talk. "I feel things happening. I am seeing things I haven't seen before. I wish I could explain it. It's like there is a ghost world around us, but not ghosts. Something else. A thin layer of fabric between this world and another one. I want to rip through it, expose what's on the other side, but I can't. Somebody will not let that happen. And that may be a good thing. I am telling you this as a friend, not as a psychiatrist. Otherwise, you would probably suggest a little hospital stay. And that cannot ever happen to me. I could not survive that. Do you understand?"

Janette nods. "Keep going."

"Have you ever heard of The Book of Enoch?" Jamey asks.

"Yes. One of the lost books of the Bible, right?" Janette replies.

"Yeah. But not really lost. Catholic Church decided it didn't like all the attention people were paying to angels; and that is mostly what Enoch is about. But there is something about this Book. In it a band of angels come to Earth and mate with women. The offspring, a race of giants, called Nephilim. God decided they must be destroyed. That's why He decided the world must be destroyed…the Great Flood. Did you know that was what the Great Flood was about? I didn't. I thought it was to destroy the sinners on this Earth that. And, to be honest, I'm not sure I remember anyway. I did it only because I thought lives were in danger. Yours, Ellie's, the new baby's. I took no pleasure in it, but feel no guilt for it. It was the right thing to do. And to be brutally honest, the pain you are feeling is not the most important thing in this deal. Your children need to live a life without fear."

Jamey goes on, "The pain you're feeling will subside over time. Other pain will replace it, other pleasure. Your kids will carry you. Maternal instinct is such an amazing thing. Wonder why God decided paternal instinct was unnecessary? I'm sure He had a good reason. Maybe it's He figures He's the only Father any of us need. Anyway, I really like Ellie. She is not your average, run-of-the-mill kid, I'm sure you know. I thought my girls were mature for their ages, but Ellie could easily be your mother, or mine. I would really like to get to know her. I would like to make her smile. I'm pretty good at that, you know."

Janette replies, "Yes, you are. You can even make me smile. Under the circumstances, that's an amazing accomplishment. Oh, just so you know, Ellie has talked non-stop about you since she met you. And the questions are endless. She thinks you're really old, but she likes you. A lot. And she has much better judgment in men than I do. She knew her father was an asshole before I did. I was always thinking everything was my fault. A typical woman reaction. As a psychiatrist I should know better. But I guess being a woman trumps being a psychiatrist. At least when it comes to dealing with your own problems.

"Now, you've made me start thinking about a 'ghost

— humans — not these Nephilim. It's even in the Bible so why don't people know this? It all sounds so fucking ridiculous. And, I'm sure you've gathered I'm not the most religious guy around. I don't even know why I'm talking about this, but I am. And I don't know why I'm talking about this to you, but I am. I think I'm losing it. I have been so sad for so long. I thought I was getting better. Working with Miguel. Carving. Creating. Living a little. I thought I was getting better. But I am not.

"And meeting you. I thought that helped. Seeing Ellie. You remind me of Connie Lee. She reminds me of my girls. It hurts — really fucking bad. And now, there's something about Dos Cruces, the entire fucking town. There is something really wrong there. Or maybe it's me. Maybe I'm what's wrong there; and here. I think I know who killed Kristin and Billy. But, I don't know how I know. It's like someone's whispering in my ear. I am not telling anyone yet. But I think I know.

"I cannot go on like this for much longer. Something has to change. I cannot endure the dreams much longer; the bad ones or the good ones. I miss my girls so much. I love them but they're not here. I miss them but I can't have them back. I will never have them back. I killed them and I should've killed myself a long time ago."

Jamey Maxwell breaks down now. He cries, for a long time. When the tears finally stop, he looks at Janette Dean. She, too, has been crying.

God placed a curse on the human race. It is not the obvious one: death. No, God disguised the curse so well, you humans think it is a blessing. You call it love.

It brings nothing but pain and sorrow. Yet you continue to seek it against the most improbable odds. And you keep finding it. Or at least you like to imagine you do.

After the tears subside, Jamey asks, "Where's Ellie?"

Janette replies, "She's not here."

Jamey looks into Janette's eyes and says, "I'm sorry for doing this to you. I don't make a habit of spilling my guts or babbling incoherently to just anyone, you know. Don't know what you do to me that makes me think it's okay to do that, but I guess I should thank you. So, thanks."

Janette says, "I just let you say what you needed to say. Now I need to say something to you. I heard from my husband's attorney and Robert has definitely filed for a divorce. And I wonder why getting a divorce, even if it's from someone you don't really like anymore, has to be so fucking painful. And, if this is painful, I cannot begin to imagine how you feel. In my case, it's just a divorce. So why does it hurt like this? Is that an obligatory reaction that society has taught us? Or is it something more? Or does it really even fucking matter? What we feel, I mean. In the great scheme of things, does it matter what individual humans feel, or think? Does it advance the evolutionary process in some way? I doubt it. I think the human race has had its time, run its course, is probably on the way out. Now, don't you wish I was your psychiatrist, Mr. Maxwell? Don't worry about me suggesting a hospital stay for you. Just look at me. Care for some coffee?"

"No thanks. I need to head back to Dos Cruces shortly. But, here's something I think I think." Jamey

continues, "Divorce is painful for a reason. If you
ly think about it, the fact that two humans, partic
ly a male and a female, ever get together in the
place is pretty amazing. Think about the game
have to play. The 'dance' we have to dance with
other. Always looking for that right word, right
right moment; the trigger. Always trying to es
get to the next stage; the next level. Then there
dynamic tension: testosterone versus estrogen. I
a lot of fucking effort and uses up a lot of energy.
trying to get into girls' pants; girls trying to kee
out. There's the going steady, the meeting the
learning all the quirks and habits. And that's
you even think about getting married. The
you're married, the quirks and habits you thou
knew, and thought were so cute, gradually bec
and annoying. Sometimes, as you know, you
they are more than just annoying quirks and
Then through some unseemly process, you h
and things seem right, for a while. My theor
when you spend so much time in physical p
with some one, especially the 'sex thing', a
exchange takes place. You literally become pa
other. So when someone leaves you, a part of
And vice-versa. Maybe there's always this s
attempt to reunite on a molecular level. Or
theory is this: maybe we're just all totally fuc

Janette's mouth smiles, but her eyes do nc
your two theories are not mutually exclusi
wish I could say thank you for your interve
my husband. I wish I knew what you said t

Jamey replies, "Trust me, you don't wa

world' or whatever," Janette continues. "I feel it too, kind of. Or something close to it. In my case, it's like someone or something else is slowly taking control. Maybe it's just stress plus depression. Now there's a wonderful fucking combination for you. Life is hard enough when everything is going just right. I am more and more amazed that most people don't wind up just killing themselves and getting it over with. Life sucks. It suck, suck, sucks. Why does it have to do that? I hope you didn't drive all the way from Dos Cruces thinking I would cheer you up," Dr. Janette Dean cracks a smile. "I do know you will find who killed Billy and Kristin; I don't know how I know, but I do.

"Oh, and one other thing: you are not wrong in Dos Cruces. And you are certainly not wrong here."

Jamey stands. Janette stands. Then Jamey takes two steps forward and embraces her. He can feel her ripening stomach against him and he remembers Connie Lee and how beautiful she was during her pregnancies. He holds Janette Dean close and feels her sobbing into his shoulder. This time, no words are spoken. After a few minutes, Jamey pulls away, turns and walks out of Janette Dean's beautiful home.

He is at St. Charles Place again. Asleep. Dreaming. Janette Dean is talking to him. He can hear her but cannot see her. She says, "I need to tell you something. I've done something really bad. Really, really bad. I'm a bad girl. Do you love me anyway?"

Then the grizzled one appears again. He says, "Wake up you damned fool. Wake up. Goddamn it, wake up!"

Unfortunately, he does.

Part IV

The Judgment

Chapter 1

And the Watchers Shall Quake

Nephilim are Godless in the purest sense of the word. They have no soul therefore they have nothing of God's.

Jamey Maxwell is back in Dos Cruces. He needs help. Big time. Before he had the angel Violet to help. Violet, of *las hermanas locas de Dos Cruces*. She told him in her own inimitable way about *Los Diablos* and what God required. But *las hermanas* have not been seen since the deaths of Luther Axelrod, Dwayne Dubois, and Jacinto "Chango" Ocala: *Los Diablos*. Violet and the ugly sister just disappeared. And in true Dos Cruces fashion, people act like they never even existed. Maybe they didn't? As far as Jamey needing help, hey, what can I say? Good help is hard to find these days.

Jamey Maxwell thinks it's about time for "the greasy skunk" prayer. This is the prayer his brother, Robert, taught him years ago. For Robert, it goes something like this: "Dear God: Please forgive me for being about the lowest living thing that can be found on this planet. I am constantly surprised that You can stand the sight of me without throwing up. I never go to church. I never pray to You unless I want something. I never appreciate the things You always do for me. I'm a lousy husband. I'm a pretty crappy father. I drink too much. I lust after women — even some of my wife's friends. I sometimes watch porn on cable. I like to gamble. I hate my job and fuck off at work a lot. I lie a lot, especially to You. Now, would You mind helping me out on a few things. If You will, I promise to try and not be a "greasy skunk" anymore. Thanks, God."

Here is Jamey's version: "Dear God: Thanks for keeping our agreement for the past forty-seven years. Thanks for punishing me now for every sin I commit on earth, so I won't have to spend an eternity in Hell. But forty-seven years, well, that's about all I can take. I realize now that I forgot to include my admission to Heaven in the deal, as I am sure You recall. I was only nine years old at the time. By the way, I don't think I've ever asked: are You in the habit of scamming naive kids on these agreements? Thanks for killing my wife and daughters; and Angelita; and Marisol; even though they did not deserve to suffer for my sins. And, yes, I am being sarcastic. So I'm sure You'll punish me for that too. Anyway, I need Your help on this undertaking. Your undertaking. So if You're not too busy or too pissed off, could You do me a favor? Thanks."

Does it make you wonder who the "greasy skunk" is in this prayer?

Well, it appears God is busy, as usual. If not busy, then how 'bout "not available." Seems to me that God is not available more and more often these days. We Watchers like to joke that God's becoming a Slacker. But we don't laugh about it anymore. Maybe He's just tired. Who knows how many seventh days He has experienced since He embarked on his "special projects?" Your Bible covers one of them.

The Bible. Oh, the Bible. Time to talk about presumptuousness again. You humans need constant reminders. How can I say this tactfully? How about this: is the entire human race out of its fucking mind? We'll talk about the Koran, the Torah, and other works of fiction, some other time. But now, the Bible.

Do any of you have a fucking clue who wrote the Bible? Do any of you have any fucking idea how many times it's been in interpreted, misinterpreted, reinterpreted, uninterpreted?

Do any of you even fucking care?

Theologians and historians think the Old Testament went like this: Genesis, Exodus, Leviticus, Numbers, and Deuteronomy. Written by Moses at the end of his life in the wilderness. No surviving witnesses. Joshua, Judges, and Ruth: maybe written during the reign of David over Israel, by unnamed, pro-David/anti-Saul, priestly historians. Psalms: King David, Moses, sons of Korah, sons of Asaph, Ethan, the Ezrahite...and several anonymous authors. Proverbs and Song of Solomon (Canticles): King Solomon, during his reign, although chapters 30 and 31 of Proverbs were supposedly written by Agur and Lemuel. Ecclesiastes: written in "the voice of the character" of King Solomon — whatever the hell that means. Isaiah, Hosea, Amos, Jonah, Micah, Nahum, and Zephaniah: self-explanatory, I guess. Samuel: anonymously written — go figure. Habakkuh and Joel: self-explanatory. Does Habakkuh even sound like a real name to you? Lamentations and Book of Jeremiah: Jeremiah, probably. Obadiah, Ezekiel, Daniel:

self-explanatory, maybe. Books of Kings: likely penned by unknown authors — ooh, what a shocker! Ezra: may have compiled both Ezra and Nehemiah and possibly Chronicles. Esther: likely written by a Persian Jew. Haggai, Zechariah, and Malachi: who the fuck knows? And you will be surprised to hear this: The Book of Job is of ambiguous origin.

Are you starting to catch my fucking drift here? No? Not yet? Well, then let's continue. New Testament: never mind. It's basically same old story. A bunch of possibly mythical, certainly maniacal old men who may, or may not, have written a bunch of incoherent, incongruent, inconsistently contradictory fairy tales.

Let's take what we have so far. And let's assume for a minute that these men actually wrote the Bible. These are men who were considered insane in their own time. Especially Paul (Saul) of Tarsus, who was considered a raving fucking maniac. These are men who if they came up to you on the street today, you would turn away making sure not to make eye contact. These are men who, in your society, would be either street people or locked up in mental institutions. Yet, not only do many of you base your lives on their writings (very loosely, I might add), but you are also betting your entire eternities on it. If God didn't think you humans were so cute, He would be really be pissed at you.

Want to see something else interesting? Want to see what went down around 363 A.D.? After a couple of hundred years of Christian scripture, a group of Catholic clergy, appointed by Pope Liberius, decided that certain literature would no longer be part of the Church — part of your Bible. It's the politics, baby!

Check it out!

Here's a partial list of books banned by the Council of Laodecia: Barnabas, I Clement, II Clement, Christ and Abgarus, The Apostles' Creed, I Hermas-Visions, II Hermas-Commands, III Hermas-Similitudes, Ephesians, I Infancy, II Infancy, Mary, Magnesians, Nicodemus, Paul and Seneca, Paul and Thecla, Philadelphians, Polycarp, Trallians, Letters of Herod and Pilate, The First Book of Adam and Eve, The Second Book of Adam and Eve, The Secrets of Enoch, The Psalms of Solomon, The Odes of Solomon, The Fourth Book of Maccabees, The Story of Ahikar, The Testament of Reuben, Asher, Joseph, Simeon, Levi, Judah, Issachar, Zebulum, Dan, Naphtali, Gad, and Benjamin.

Think about it: these books were just as much a part of Christianity as the books contained in your current Old and New Testaments. But, humans, not your God, arbitrarily and I'm sure, capriciously, decided they were no longer relevant. The Secrets of Enoch (The Book of Enoch) was among these, and obviously, thanks to me you have now heard of it. But have you ever even fucking heard of most of the other books? Couple of them? Any of them? Didn't think so.

Then there was The Book of Jubilees. The one book that actually attempted to explain the biggest logic problem in the Bible. And let me tell you, even though you do not want to hear it, there are *mucho* logic problems in the Bible. None greater, however, than the problem with how humans actually did "go forth and multiply." The Bible tells you that Adam and Eve had three sons. Abel, Cain, and Seth. Then suddenly Cain has a wife. Hmmm. How did that happen? Oh, wait, I know, God works in mysterious ways. Doesn't quite cut it here. So, The Book of Jubilees gives us the answer. And what a fucking soap opera answer it is. Seems that Adam and Eve had nine children, including several daughters. Seems that Cain married his sister. And, hell, he wasn't even from Alabama. Now, even in the fourth century incest was taboo. So it seems the church fathers decided The Book of Jubilees was just a pack of friggin' lies. Cause ain't no way God be lettin' no incest be goin' on. By the way, in its time The Book of Jubilees was the equivalent of a New York Times bestseller. You humans love your stories of lust and perversion. You love to be shocked. Of course you must deny that you love your erotica. Wouldn't be proper. Give me a fucking break. You ignore the flaws, the contradictions, the illogical fables of the Book which you think will somehow magically and mysteriously bestow eternal bliss upon you. You humans are some ring-tail-tooters.

Guess what else these Catholic clergy did at the Council of Laodecia? They totally fucked up your week-ends. How, you ask? Read Canon 29 (of 60): "Christians must not judaize by resting on the Sabbath, but must work on that day, rather honouring the Lord's Day; and, if they can, resting then as Christians. But if any shall be found to be judaizers, let them be anathema from Christ."

Up until this time, Jews and Christians got to sit on their collective ass on Saturday and Sunday. And guess what the penalty for violating Canon 29 was? Death. I'm telling you, the Council of Laodecia really fucked up your weekends.

Now just for fun, let's talk about the twelve apostles and I'll keep this simple. Let's just talk about how they died:

1. St. Peter: crucified, upside down, by Nero in Rome.
2. St. Andrew: crucified in Greece on a transverse cross.
3. St James the Greater: beheaded in Jerusalem.
4. St. Phillip: crucified in Phrygia.
5. St. Bartholomew: flayed alive in Armenia.
6. St. Thomas: pierced with a lance in Persia.
7. St. Matthew: beheaded in Ethiopia.
8. St. James the Lesser: clubbed to death in Jerusalem.
9. St. Jude: axed to death in Persia.
10. St. Simon: sawed into pieces in Mesopotamia.
11. St. Matthias: pierced with a lance in southern Asia.
12. St. John: the exception; died of old age in Ephesus.

Question: With these itineraries and the terminal consequences, are you having second thoughts about God being your travel agent through life?

One other thing: word on the street is God took Enoch directly to Heaven; none of that pesky "dying" thing. Enoch got to "pass go" and "collect $200." What was that about?

Chapter 2

And for the Godless There Shall be a Curse

The oldest white woman in Dos Cruces is driving the oldest Cadillac in Dos Cruces. But Mrs. Welhausen isn't going anywhere. Somehow she missed the turn to Dos Cruces Mercantile by 30 yards and 30 years. The old emporium has been boarded up for that long. And the old woman missed the road by that far. Consequently, she is now stuck high-center on the Union Pacific railroad track. The Cadillac's back wheels are spinning futilely. Mrs. Welhausen is still moving the steering wheel back and forth, oblivious to the fact she is stranded and in mortal danger. The train will soon be coming through town.

The crazy train director is very confused. He is used to throwing rocks at the trains as they pass. He is not sure what to do about the Cadillac. He goes with his instincts. The rocks start flying, clinking and pinging off the car.

Jamey, Daniel, and Taz see the old lady's Caddy and the train director. Jamey looks at Taz with a tired smile. Taz reciprocates. Jamey feels a little bit like Dudley Do-Right. Time to go get Ms. Nell off the tracks. Looks like

Snidely Whiplash has struck again.

They pull up beside Mrs. Welhausen and Jamey gets out of the old blue S-10. He yells at the train director, *"Ándele! Vamos a la casa!"* The train director looks disappointed. He was just trying to do his job. But he follows Jamey's instructions and heads for his mother's house.

Jamey walks over to the Caddy and taps on the driver's window. The old lady looks through the glass and wonders how this young fellow can be keeping up with her car.

Jamey keeps tapping until she rolls down the window. "Ma'am, you're stuck on the railroad track."

"What?" asks Mrs. Welhausen, trying to focus through the dark coke bottle eyeglasses. Along with being pretty much blind, she is pretty much deaf.

"You're going to have to get out of the car, ma'am. The train will be through shortly," Jamey says gently but firmly. "You're stuck on the tracks."

"Oh no," the old lady mumbles. "Please don't tell my husband. I'm not supposed to drive anymore. I just needed to get some bread and eggs at the store." Mrs. Welhausen was trying to drive down memory lane to a ghost store. She was probably going to visit her ghost husband too. Mr. Welhausen died 10 years ago.

Jamey Maxwell finally convinces the old woman that she is, in fact, stuck on the tracks. He walks her over to the closest shade tree and tells Daniel and Taz to stay with her. Jamey then goes to find a few *batos* to help lift the front end of the dinosaur Caddy off the rail. He finds just what he needs at "Batos 'R Us," also known as Reyes Bar.

Within five minutes Jamey, Daniel, and five strong

young men in various stages of inebriation hoist the ancient Cadillac off the Union Pacific railroad tracks. About three minutes before the San Antonio/Laredo southbound hits Dos Cruces. As Jamey's dad, St. Charles, would have said, "It was nick and tuck there for awhile."

Each ten bucks richer thanks to Jamey Maxwell, the five young men head back to Reyes Cafe to hoist *cerveza de Miller*. They have hoisted lots of metal today. Steel and aluminum. They laugh as one says, "man, if the old *gringa* keeps driving, we can retire soon." The other four reply, "*Salud!*" The festivities continue.

Jamey drives the old lady back to her once nice *gringa* home, now in the latter stages of terminal neglect. He takes the keys next door to her neighbor's house and tells Mrs. Bustamante what happened. She helps take care of the old white woman. Mrs. Bustamante nods her head in complete understanding and says, "*Gracias*."

Jamey Maxwell walks back to his truck. Daniel and Taz are waiting. The three of them continue their journey to Miguel Veras' workshop. Life in Dos Cruces goes on. Echoes of hollow laughter. Smiles without joy. *Vida sin sentido*.

I always wanted to be human. You are God's favorite you know. Sometimes I feel like God interspersed human genes with angel genes when creating me. Maybe just for His enjoyment. Just for His amusement. He does get so fucking bored, it seems. I hate Him — because I love Him.

God's horror movie is beginning to come together inside Jamey Maxwell's brain. The characters are becoming defined, the plot becoming clearer. He's also getting a quick glimpse of coming attractions. Jamey wishes he would have killed himself several years ago.

Again, the phone rings at St. Charles Place. Jamey answers. "Mr. Maxwell, this is Luis Moya. I hope I'm not bothering you."

"Not at all," Jamey replies. He has learned there is such a thing as 'good' bothered. Jamey Maxwell realizes he has been waiting for this call.

"I think I may have found something. I went back to the place where the Garnetts' bodies were found. Then backtracked where I thought the killer, or killers, would have come and gone. He or they did a good job of erasing their tracks. Plus most of the area is solid rock. But I walked several hundred yards in a couple of directions and finally stumbled on a white tag — it's one of those tags found on bags at a feed store. It's from a feed store in Kerrville. Name of the place is Hill Country Farm and Ranch Supply. I'm taking this to Earl McVay in a little while, but thought you might be interested too. I'm not telling anyone I told you," Luis finishes.

"Can you give me all the information on the tag? Feed type, ingredients, whatever?" Jamey asks.

"Of course," Luis replies. And spends the next few minutes reciting ingredients for premium horse feed.

It seems that, unfortunately for Brad and Vanessa Scofield, a little detail was "overlooked." A "fly in the ointment" as some humans are wont to say. When unloading the bodies of Billy and Kristin on the Galvan Ranch in almost total darkness, they also deposited a little piece of evidence. Those feed bags they covered the bodies with — well, one of them had a tag that just happened to come loose — and then it just happened to stick to the plastic bag in which Billy was wrapped. And then it just happened to fall to the hard ground on the Galvan Ranch. And it just happened that neither Brad nor Vanessa noticed it. After all that impeccable planning and scheming too. And it just happened that Luis Moya had an overwhelming urge to go back to the crime scene and look around. And once there, it just happened that he had an inclination to walk in just a certain direction. It's funny how shit "just happens" sometimes.

Jamey Maxwell wastes no time. Within minutes of talking to Luis Moya, Jamey is on the phone with Tom Respondek, manager of Kerr County Farm and Ranch Supply.

"That is a specialty horse feed we mix right here on site. We have three serious horse breeders in the county that use it. It's a little pricey but they all can afford it…uh, and it's worth every penny," Tom Respondek explains.

Jamey asks for the names of the three horse breeders. "Well, there's Anderson Farms, Scofield Ranch, and the XO Ranch. That's it," Tom answers. Jamey thanks him.

"What else can I help you with Mr. St. Michael? You in the horse "bidness" yourself? If you're looking for that edge, we'd be glad to cook you up a batch of our best." Tom Respondek is being the good salesman that he is. But he hears only silence on the other end of the line. Then a dial tone. Dead air.

Jamey Maxwell drives to Miguel's workshop. He finds the old man inside working on his carving of *La Virgen de Guadalupe*. The carving is almost finished. Daniel is sweeping the sawdust and wood chips. Taz is sitting up and looking at Jamey with his eerily intelligent dog eye. Taz seems to know "what up?"

Miguel does not look up from his carving. He just says, "*Bueno... ya es hora*?"

Jamey says, "Yes, I think it's time Miguel Angelo. Miguel Angelo — Michelangelo — a term of endearment which sounds bittersweet to the old *santero* now. It sounds like the end is beginning. It sounds like he will soon lose another person; another loved one. Miguel is weary of the losing.

Losing. Another word to sum up the lives of humans. Losing losers. That's what you are. But you just fucking keep going, don't you? I guess for you it boils down to this: what's the alternative? Being creative, you may even have invented an alternative, literally, and you call it "Heaven." You believe you will be rewarded for your losing. Loveable losing losers, that's what you are. And maybe, just maybe, you will. Or not. You humans love your mysteries, so far be it for me to ruin it for you. One of several things will happen when you die: 1) Nothing; 2) Heaven; 3) Hell; 4) Something else. So, it's still a mystery, right? I like mysteries too.

But let's be more specific and speak of Miguel Vera's losing. It did not stop when he lost his beautiful wife, Graciela, in 1965. In 1968, his oldest son, Marcos, who had just turned eighteen, was killed in a ridiculously unnecessary war amongst humans in a place you call Viet-Nam. I guess the question to ask: is there such a thing as a necessary war? The answer is "yes and no." The no would refer to wars on your planet.

Miguel had not recovered from the death of his beloved Graciela. He had no way of dealing with the death of his oldest son. So he carved. And he carved, prolifically, for the next year or so. Then, in 1970, his youngest son, Lucas, killed himself. Lucas was seventeen. A sensitive boy who had lost his mother as an infant. Then he lost his brother, his hero. Life became too much for Lucas Veras before his life had even really begun. Miguel carved relentlessly. And as Miguel became ever more despondent, his carvings became ever more beautiful. There is no irony to be found here.

Then it was just Miguel and his middle son, Mathias. Soon it was just Miguel. Mathias left Dos Cruces when he was nineteen. He went to California to live with uncles, aunts, nephews, nieces. He found escape, as many young humans do, in drugs. He found acceptance, as many young humans do, by joining a gang. He was killed in a drive-by shooting in 1972. He was nineteen. Mathias, Lucas, Marcos — none of Miguel's sons made it to their twentieth birthdays.

At this point, Miguel was beyond disconsolate. He blamed God, and rightfully so. As with everything, God could have intervened and left Miguel with something; someone. It was almost as if God was punishing Miguel for carving graven images. Even though Miguel did it out of his love for his God. There is *mucha* irony to be found here.

Since that time Miguel has capitulated. He has forgiven God. I am not sure God has reciprocated.

Jamey Maxwell gets in his little blue S-10 pickup and heads for San Antonio. Specifically, he heads for the exquisitely pretentious residence of Brad and Vanessa Scofield.

Let me say that I have judged Vanessa Scofield guilty of the crime of pretentiousness, presumptuousness' ugly cousin. And in my opinion, she should be punished for this just as she should be punished for being a cold-blooded murderess.

Again, no prior notice. He hopes to catch them off-guard, although he doubts Vanessa Scofield is ever totally off-guard. Brad, Jamey believes, will be a different story.

He pulls up in front of the Scofield's Alamo Heights home. Alamo Heights is where all of the old money of San Antonio resides. The new money has moved north to the Dominion area near Boerne. Old money tends to be traditional, conservative, cautious. Old money likes to stay in one place as long as possible.

The exterior of the Scofield house reeks of old money. Rather elegant. It's the interior that is over-the-top. A classic case of a middle-class girl who has hit the nuptial jackpot and is out to show the world. Vanessa has little taste but *mucha* ambition. Angry ambition, at that. When Jamey rings the doorbell and is cautiously allowed inside by Brad, he witnesses *las aspiraciones con mucha furia*. Aspiration *con* anger is a powerful combination. The interior of the Scofield home, Vanessa's home, appears to have been decorated by the illegitimate spawn of Adolph Hitler and Liberace. Gay Hitler, indeed. There are crystal chandeliers everywhere, including the bathrooms. Red toile wallpaper, no doubt quite pricey, assaults the eyes. Red toile fabric covers large, overstuffed sofas and chairs. It's as if some virulent and terminal form of upholstery cancer has spread to the furniture, leaving giant cushiony toile tumors in its wake. Jamey has the notion that Vanessa searched worldwide for red toile carpet, but had to settle for the solid, clotted blood color instead.

Jamey explains why he is here. He is looking into the

murders of Billy and Kristin Garnett on behalf of the family. He tells Brad Scofield that he has been told that Vanessa and Kristin were good friends. He asks if Vanessa is around. Brad looks warily, and wearily, at Jamey Maxwell and says, "No, she's out shopping but she should be home shortly." Jamey is glad he caught Brad Scofield alone. He believes this could be fruitful.

"I don't know? Maybe you should come back..." Brad's answer trails off. He has already lost the battle to keep Jamey Maxwell from intruding into his life. Brad Scofield is not a strong person.

"Brad, can I call you Brad?" Before Bradley Scofield has a chance to answer, Jamey asks, "Brad, how well did you know Kristin and Billy?"

Brad, displaying the look of a guy receiving an enema with a garden hose, says, "We...well, we were friends, as a couple, that is. Vanessa and Kristin were friends from high school. I was in the Key Club with Kristin and she introduced me to Vanessa. Billy and I were more or less casual acquaintances. We knew each other through Kristin and Vanessa."

"When was the last time you saw them, Brad?" asks Jamey. Jamey has an overwhelming urge to say "Brad" a lot. He thinks this will confuse Brad just enough to become even more stupid.

"It, it was several months ago, I think. Yeah, I guess it was at a Daughters of the Tejas Legacy fundraiser. Vanessa was thinking about joining. I'm not sure if she did or not."

"Do you remember exactly when that was, Brad?"

"No. Vanessa will. She never forgets anything." Brad says this with just a touch of disgust, which Jamey zeroes in on.

"I think that's a wife thing, Brad. They have incredible memories, especially when a husband screws up," Jamey smiles as he baits Brad.

"Ain't that the fuckin' truth? I'm not sure who invented marriage, but I hope they had to suffer as much as the rest of us. It probably was a woman, anyway." Brad's caution is starting to fade.

"Well, it's a good thing that guys like you and me never fuck up. Right, Brad?"

"I wish. According to Vanessa, I fuck up pretty much daily. Or hourly." Brad is zoning out.

"Really? You look like a guy that would never get caught fucking up, Brad."

Brad snaps to and looks Jamey Maxwell in the eyes, but only for a second. He then looks down and mumbles something.

"What was that, Brad?"

"Nothing," Brad replies. "Vanessa will be home any time now. Maybe she can answer your questions. I…I really don't know anything…that can help…"

"You have already helped me Brad," Jamey replies. Brad feels very gloomy.

"I have? How's that?" Brad says, wishing he could shut the fuck up. He just can't though.

"Just letting me in your house has helped, Brad."

Brad looks into Jamey Maxwell's eyes again. This time he sees the reflection of a guy that has just totally screwed the pooch.

"Did you enjoy killing them, Brad?" Jamey asks flatly.

"Wha…what are you talking about?" Brad is experiencing the fight or flight syndrome, but neither is an option for him at this point.

"Did you get to 'enjoy' Kristin before you killed her?"

"Shut up! I'm not talking to you anymore. You need to get out of my house…or I'll…"

"Or you'll what, Brad? Call the police? How 'bout I do that for you?"

Brad starts to turn but Jamey Maxwell grabs his arm and pulls him close, looks into Brad's coward eyes and says, "I'm going to kill you, Brad. And your wife. I'm going to kill her first so you can watch. Not because I think you care if she dies. I just want you to watch her suffer so you know what's gonna happen to you. I want you to experience a little of what Billy and Kristin felt. God wants you to suffer Brad. You want to know how I know that? He told me."

Brad's bodily functions have gone on autopilot. He has simultaneously pissed and shit his pants. He is sweating. He is crying. Fluids are evacuating every orifice of his body.

"Vanessa will be home anytime now," Brad sobs. "Talk to her. She can explain. I didn't do anything…she told me to…I couldn't help it…"

"Do you want to know how I'm going to kill you and Vanessa, Brad? Do you want me to describe it to you? Do you want to tell you what Hell is gonna be like for you? I know. God told me." Jamey whispers with the timbre of a madman. Then, without another word, Jamey Maxwell turns and walks out.

Can we please talk about Enoch again? Pretty please? *Con azúcar?* Most humans have never heard of Enoch. He is first mentioned in the Bible in Genesis 5.

Jude quotes Enoch in Hebrews 11. But where did Jude, where does anyone, find the words of Enoch? The answer is in The Book of Enoch. And just who was Enoch? Noah's grandfather for starters.

The Book of Enoch is considered apocryphal, that is, fictional, by most of your so-called scholars. And although it was written centuries before the coming of your Messiah, it speaks of many tenets on which your Christianity is built. In fact, early Christians took it as scripture, their literature littered with references ascribed to Enoch and his little fucking book. Then, as we've discussed earlier, in the fourth century A.D., the Council of Laodicea decided The Book of Enoch was a load of crap. Or at least that's what they said. This, however, was not the real reason they wanted to bring into disrepute this quaint little masterpiece. In at least this one case, they were not capricious. Do you want to know why it became discredited? Because of us. Yes, us. Angels. Too much talk about angels. Angel worship=idolatry. Enoch had seen us; had talked to us; then he had the fucking nerve to write about us; and, of course, this piqued everyone's curiosity about us. Humans were starting to get a little too attached; showing a little too much interest in angels. The church fathers had become jealous of us. How ironic is that? Since God is constantly admonishing, punishing us Watchers for our jealousy of humans? Maybe it was part of that "God works in mysterious ways" bullshit. Maybe it was His doing. Anyway, after being under the ban of the authorities for many years, it gradually passed out of circulation. I think, just maybe, The Book of Enoch is ready for a major fucking comeback.

Chapter 3

And the Children of Fornication Shall be Destroyed

To me, it doesn't seem fair that God allowed the Nephilim to be created and now He insists that they be destroyed. This has been a topic of conversation amongst us Angels for eons. Here is our collective conclusion: God doesn't give a shit if it's fair or not.

The word "forsaken" comes to mind. Forsaken. Such a beautiful word. It's my second favorite word in the English language. The aforementioned 'fuck' being my favorite. Synonyms for forsaken include abandoned, desolate, isolated, vacant, empty. All of these words could be used to describe the Nephilim. They could also be used to describe Jamey Maxwell, Janette Dean, Kristin and Billy Garnett, along with the entire human race. And the past tense of my favorite word could also be used for all of the above: 'fucked'.

By the way, if humans were made in God's own image, where did you get your sense of humor? Certainly not from Him. And while we're at it, let me tell you this: you don't look a thing like God.

For the first time in many years, probably since his early days of marriage, Jamey Maxwell had a wet dream last night. A nocturnal emission. To him, it was not only messy, it was completely irrelevant. As he woke, the dream was dissipating. And, as most dreams are, especially erotic ones, it was fragmentary and illogical. The smell of spilt semen reminded him of his childhood, when he was still uncorrupted. It smelled like the starch his mother used to cook on the top of the stove, before the invention of the spray variety. Unfortunately, it also reminded him of the love of his life, gone now. He wondered why men smelled like some industrial by-product and women smelled like some lovely secret of nature. He missed the scent of Connie Lee's bodily fluids mixed with his, mitigating the corruption. For the first time in many years, it made him doubt God's existence. For why would God be so petty, as to use a wet dream, a nocturnal emission, to remind him of his loss? Of his sorrow? Jamey gets up and cleans himself.

His mind has turned to his beloved daughters, Julie and Josie. The pain of losing them is fresh again. For a brief moment, he pictures them there with him. But he is unable to hold on to the vision. His grip on life is tenuous now and he is able to focus on one thing only: the killing of Brad and Vanessa Scofield. I cannot afford to let his mind drift elsewhere. It is time.

Things happen in your world. Life happens. Shit happens. Death happens. Humans are born. And then they die. In between, they spend their days trying to make a connection. They call this connection many things: family, friendship, sex, love. It's all an illusion, except for the love a mother has for her children. That is all God ever gave most of you. For some not even that. Jamey Maxwell, for example. Everything else you humans have is just made up. Somewhere along the line, you developed a very active imagination. God did not plan that, but He doesn't care. *No le hace.*

Here is something most of you never see, even though it is right before your eyes. On the vellum of your life there is watermark. For each human there exists a separate page and a watermark which is unique. It is so faint, so subtle. Virtually imperceptible. There are two exceptions: you see it the moment you are born and the moment you die. Helpless and hopeless moments. God occasionally grants special dispensation and allows us Seraphs to show you while you can actually understand it. In Jamey Maxwell's life, I am that watermark. The watermark is darkening now.

Chapter 4

And They Shall Find No Mercy

Bradley and Vanessa Scofield must die. It is God's will. But not for the obvious reasons. Before I reveal God's plan, you will have to humor me. You will have to be patient.

Jamey Maxwell, again, is the avenging deputy angel. A reluctant one, of course. And yet again, it is not optional. He gets in his truck and heads north to San Antonio.

He calls Scott Stephenson and asks him to meet at the International House of Pancakes on Interstate 10 near Scott and Kay Stephenson's lovely, sad house. Jamey tells Scott to come alone.

Jamey Maxwell sits at the booth at IHOP looking at the menu and his mind begins to stray. If Jesus Christ were alive on this Earth today, would He and His disciples have a Last Brunch here? And if they did, would one of the disciples, say Judas Iscariot, the son of perdition, order the Rooty Tooty Fresh and Fruity Combo? And would that be the sign of betrayal? Jamey Maxwell is a very sick man.

Now Scott Stephenson is here at the International

House of Pancakes. He walks to the booth. Jamey stands to greet him, but neither says a word. They speak through the eyes of two people sharing the most profound and tragic bond which can be found on your planet. Through the eyes of two fathers who have lost their daughters, their beloved daughters, too young.

Then they sit. But only for a moment before Jamey Maxwell says these words: "True justice in this world is rare. Revenge without consequence is virtually non-existent. You and your wife will have both. Ask God to let it sustain you." With that, Jamey gets up and walks out of the International House of Pancakes. Scott Stephenson watches realizing this is a man he will never see or hear from again.

Jamey Maxwell returns to the Scofield home in Alamo Heights. It is 2:30 in the morning. Jamey breaks a small window leading to the laundry room. It is on the opposite side of the house from the master bedroom. He does this rather quietly, but is not all that worried about waking Brad and Vanessa. He believes God is on his side and he, of course, is right. The truth is, he does not care if he gets caught or killed. Jamey Maxwell is weary. Eternal oblivion sounds pretty fucking good to him.

Ever since Jamey's visit with Brad three weeks ago, Brad and Vanessa have been rather paranoid. They could not turn to the police for protection, obviously. For a week they hired a security guard to park in front of their home all night long. But after looking out on several occasions and seeing the old guy asleep in his car, they decided maybe their $400 per night was not being well spent. After two weeks, their paranoia began to subside a bit. Too bad. Big mistake. They should have put as a reminder above their bed the poster which says, "Just Because You're Paranoid, It Doesn't Mean They're Not Out To Get You."

Vanessa, who has such an affinity for plotting and executing murders, does not have a clue how to prevent herself, and her pussy-whipped, brain-dead husband, from being murdered. Now, there's some irony for you.

Here's the deal: Humans are prostitutes. All of you. You always have been and always will be. But, it is not your fault. It is God's plan. Remember, as a Watcher, I've been around *todo el tiempo*. I've seen you in action since Day 6. Humans are whores. I can already hear the outcry, the denial, the anger. Get over it. Live with it.

For now, let's talk about female prostitutes. Vanessa Scofield is your poster girl.

When humans first populated the Earth, women were used almost exclusively for sex and treated as chattel. Good example: in ancient Greece, priestesses of the temples were expected to fellate all the men that entered daily, often in the hundreds, to maintain their favored status. Fast forward thousands of years. Look at your television, your movies, your magazines, your billboards. Look how your young girls dress. Look whom they emulate: Britney Spears; Christina Aguilera, Janet Jackson. Look at your reality television shows: "Who Wants to Marry a Millionaire;" "For Love or Money;" "The Bachelorette;" etceteras. Prehistoric woman gave up her freedom, her identity, her life, for sex. At least she had an excuse: she would not have survived otherwise. Now, you give it up for money, for creature comforts, for stuff. If you are lucky, you will have to fellate only a few dozen guys before you find the one that goes "ka-ching, ka-ching." Women: oh that voodoo that you do is such doo doo. You try to justify it. You try to rationalize it. You try to call it love. Whatever.

Speaking of whatever; for whatever it's worth, I love women. Most of them anyway. There is one very current exception.

And don't even get me started on men.

Jamey casually walks through the dark house without hesitation. He does not need to see where he is going. God is leading the way. Now he is at the foot of Brad's and Vanessa's designer California king-sized bed. In the darkness, Jamey Maxwell softly delivers God's words: "I am here."

Vanessa wakes first and screams. "Brad, wake up…someone's in the room!"

Brad, a sound sleeper, groggily asks, "What the fuck? Oh my God, it's him!" What the fuck, indeed.

Jamey Maxwell fires a round from his Smith and Wesson Model 59 into the headboard. Vanessa again screams. Brad urinates.

"Who's there? What do you want? I have money in my purse, take it!" Vanessa pleads in the darkness. "Please don't hurt us!"

"It's him Vanessa! He's gonna kill us now! I told you, you stupid fucking bitch!" Brad shouts and begins to sob.

Gradually Brad's and Vanessa's eyes adjust to the gloom and make out the shape of the man at the end of their expensive bed. His silence is infinitely more menacing than the gunshot.

Then out of nowhere, it strikes. A guardian angel. A shadow, a specter, a phantom. But it has weight. It has mass. Although only temporary, for it takes great effort for a beast such as this (and guardian angels are nothing more) to materialize. It strikes Jamey Maxwell in the dark, knocking him to the floor. Jamey is not surprised for he is but an automaton now. Rising to his feet, he fires a round into the amorphous shape. To no avail. The beast strikes Jamey again, but I catch my protégé before he falls. I have intervened. But I am not alone in my intervention. The "dog" Taz, unbeknownst to Jamey, hopped in the back of the little blue truck when Jamey left Dos Cruces, and made the terminal trip too. I cannot always see the dog. Another blind spot and God's doing for sure. But I see him now. He has the guardian angel by the crotch and is silently ripping and tearing. I hate the dog, but so admire him. The dog hates me, but so loves Jamey Maxwell.

Now this guardian angel, this monster, is moaning and beginning to panic. Because these cretins' biggest fear is that they will die like the humans around them (which, unfortunately, will never happen) I say these words in Aramaic: "What is this that rests not? The Lord of the Spirits, the Lord that separates the light and the darkness, commands you to return to your shadow dwelling or the worms shall be your bed. Go now!" The beast is gone. And so am I. Taz is left ripping and tearing at ghostly testicles. The dog has gone temporarily insane with rage.

Brad and Vanessa, now in shock and scared, but not shitless, witness this spontaneous turmoil in the darkness. They see the shifting shapes. They hear the gunshot. They hear the voice speaking in tongues. But, they have not a clue what has just transpired. Jamey Maxwell knows precisely what has gone down. Knows precisely "what up?" He is no longer living in his old world. He has crossed over.

The last thing Brad Scofield sees in this world is the teeth of a small dog, possessed by God, before they latch on to Brad's abominably superficial face.

The killings — the well-deserved killings — of Brad and Vanessa Scofield were shocking in their brutality and callousness. Man, did they ever fucking reap what they fucking sowed. Jamey Maxwell does not remember the details of these killings, but knows that he has killed…again. His conscience does not allow him to dwell on this. In fact, this part of his conscience, the part which would make him hesitate before wreaking vengeance upon those who deserve it, no longer exists. It has been metaphysically removed by the Giver of All Consciences.

Chapter 5

And They Shall Be Cast Into Darkness

Again, Manuelito smells the stench of death. This time, he instantly knows what and where. This time, he finds the two bodies in the exact spot as the last two. This time, he doesn't cry. This time, he falls to his knees, raises his face to heaven, and promises God he will join the priesthood — tomorrow. He wishes it could be sooner. He will do anything to keep from finding any more dead bodies.

Time has passed. It has been a month since the bodies of Vanessa and Brad Scofield were found on the Galvan Ranch near Langtry. Jamey Maxwell has been back in Dos Cruces working with the old *santero* since then. The San Antonio Police Department has been working on this high profile case, but do not really have much to go on. It's strange, the crime was so violent and messy, you would think there would be all sorts of evidence to be found. But by the time the homicide detectives arrived at the Scofield house, there was nary a clue. And when the "Three Stooges and a Texas Ranger" arrived at the crime scene — the now redundant crime scene — in Torres County, ditto on the evidence. Have I mentioned that God works in mysterious ways?

Jamey has been feeling much better; the nightmares coming less frequently. Daniel and Taz are a source of peace. Miguel, a reservoir of strength and unspoken love, cannot believe he still has Jamey Maxwell in his life. He was certain that he was losing him. And, in his *corazón viejo*, Miguel is hoping he will leave this Earth before the last two people he has left to love: Jamey Maxwell and Daniel Galvan.

Jamey's work at Miguel's side has been, well, rewarding. He has carved a beautiful rendition of San Miguel. Saint Michael, the Archangel. To the mesquite carving he has added a tin crown, a wood and tin sword, wood and tin scales. He has placed the carving on a wooden base with scalloped and punched tin nailed to the circumference. Saint Michael's vestments are painted in bright colors: reds, cobalt blue, touches of teal and orange. What should have turned out gaudy instead turned out tasteful. Refined. As if all the excesses of brilliant colors have somehow counteracted, neutralized, each other. The overall result is the perfect combination of skill, compassion, and absolution (real or imagined, *no le hace*).

He has been in touch with Janette Dean by phone several times a week. She is usually the one to call. Ever since his trip with Luis Moya to Seminole Canyon, Jamey has been thinking about returning to experience the rugged beauty, the enviable serenity. Until this moment, he has planned on going alone. Now he finds himself saying, "Hey, you female psychiatrist, you. Would you like to go on a West Texas picnic?"

"I'm not much of an outdoor girl, but what the hell, sure," she answers. Jamey Maxwell senses something strange in Dr. Dean's voice. And the voice inside Jamey's head flashes an ominous warning, but it's brief and he's had enough of ominous warnings. Instead, he gives her the details and picks her up two days later. It is a warm but overcast Monday. Now July, it will be hot when they get to Seminole Canyon. But neither one of them cares about that. They are both just looking for respite. He plans on taking her to Paint Cave. He wants her to see the petroglyphs.

On the drive westward, the conversation between Jamey Maxwell and Janette Dean turns to the topic which intimately connects them: depression. Dr. Dean begins, "I've quit taking new patients. I've also transferred all of my patients, except for those diagnosed with depression, to my associates. And I took the last week off. I've blamed it on my pregnancy, but that's a lie.

"I have come up with a new, and in my case, a last ditch approach to treating depression. It has no medical basis. As far as I know, I'm the only psychiatrist and maybe the only person in the world who has come up with this particular theory. In fact, I will probably be disbarred when the truth comes out. It's only a matter of time. I don't care about that anymore. I'm very tired. Weary."

Jamey listens. Janette continues, "My theory, my belief is this: there are two and only two common traits in those who suffer from depression. The first is, they all have dreams, imaginings, longings. Dreams that equal salvation, at least here on Earth. Dreams about becoming a writer; becoming an artist; quitting a time-wasting, soul-killing job; finding a secluded place in the country; escaping the cruel realities of the world. These dreams keep them going. The second is, they all have a "fall back" position — a contingency plan. A plan for what they will do in a worst case scenario. And almost without exception, that plan is suicide." Jamey nods, for Dr. Janette Dean has just hit the proverbial nail on the proverbial head.

Janette continues, "But the real tragedy is this. Family, and even friends, think the dream is the problem. They want this person to live in the 'real world'. They spend a great amount of energy and time trying to take away the dream. And they spend virtually no energy or time addressing the fall-back position. This is, no doubt, a recipe for disaster. I believe most suicides are a result of these two simultaneous approaches by the well-meaning. So, now I encourage family members of my patients to meet with me, but many of them refuse to participate. Those cases I consider hopeless. They will end in tragedy. To those loved ones who do meet with me, I say: Do not try to take away this person's dream under any circumstances. In fact, embrace the dream. Make it part of the relationship. Even if you know that this dream may never be realized. And, secondly, I tell them the patient has a fall-back position, virtually guaranteed to be suicide — slow or fast. Many of the loved ones have never even considered this. I ask them to work with me in modifying the fall-back position. To transform the fall- back plan from suicide to something less permanent.

Surprisingly, homelessness is the most commonly agreed upon alternative. Once the patient replaces thoughts of suicide with the possibility of living the life of the homeless, you can see a burden lift before your very eyes. But this works only if you allow the dream. Take away the dream and there is only one fall-back position."

Dr. Dean is suddenly quiet. For the next thirty minutes these two depressed souls contemplate the empty West Texas landscape.

"And as far as drugs, anti-depressants, go," Janette suddenly erupts, "all I can say is, 'fuck 'em.'" At this moment, Jamey Maxwell has an epiphany. Someone has taken away, someone has obliterated, Janette Dean's dream. And her fall-back position is not homelessness.

There was a father. A good father. In fact, a most wonderful father. He loved his children with such passion. He loved his children with such intensity. But his love was not unconditional. Oh no, far from it. The condition his children were required to meet to continue to receive his fervent love was this: total obedience. The children had to obey him to the exclusion of everyone, everything. The penalty for disobedience was harsh, inhumane, in fact, horrendous. For the noncompliant child, the punishment was unrelenting torture of the most heinous nature, unspeakable. Now, in most human societies, a father such as this would be branded a callous criminal, beyond rehabilitation. Beyond redemption. He would be incarcerated and probably killed behind bars, as child abusers are the most despised of the prison caste. Now, for the irony of all ironies ever conceived: in most human societies, this is the Father you choose to pattern your life after; that you fall to your knees to worship; that you pray to for your own salvation. You call him God, Yahweh, Allah. Of all the mysteries of humankind, I find this one "takes the cake." Maybe one of you can explain it to me sometime. But, I doubt it.

Oh yes, I almost forgot: your God, my God, is also a mass murderer and a serial killer.

Janette Dean says, "Ellie is much better now." The words seem random and sound hollow. Jamey Maxwell starts to reply, but cannot. His mind is momentarily blank. They drive on in silence.

As they approach Lake Amistad, Janette looks out the window at the ruggedly beautiful shoreline and the whitecaps on the lake. "What do think of God?" she asks.

Jamey replies, "I don't think you will believe it."

"Try me," Janette responds.

"I love Him. For no particular reason."

"I believe you. I don't love Him. I don't know who He is. But I do know He is powerful. Either that, or the entire fucking world is delusional. Before there was one God, there were many gods. Humans were determined to have at least one I guess. Why do you think you love Him?"

Jamey answers, "I don't have a fucking clue."

Janette asks, "Does He ever make you do things you don't want to do?"

"Yes," Jamey replies. "But I don't want to talk about it."

"Okay, I was just asking." She starts to quietly sob.

"I'm sorry. Why do you ask? Does He do that to you, too?"

"Yes," Janette replies. "But I don't want to talk about it."

Jamey doesn't know whether to laugh or keep his mouth shut. He decides on the latter. Janette Dean, he tells himself, is not in a joking mood.

They leave Lake Amistad behind. After a while, Janette says, "I think He knows what He's doing. I have to believe that. I have nothing else left to believe."

She continues, "He talks to me now. Maybe I should try to love Him. Might as well, I don't think He's going to stop talking to me. I wish He would though. It makes me very tired."

"I know," replies Jamey Maxwell.

Janet asks, "Do ever wonder what if it's not God talking?"

"No, never, "Jamey says.

Then all is quiet again.

Janette and Jamey arrive at Seminole Canyon State Park. Jamey talks to the same Park Manager that he and Luis Moya had talked to before. The Park Manager gives him and Janette permission to hike to Paint Cave. The manager gives Jamey directions to a park road normally off-limits which will take them within a few hundred yards of the cave. Jamey is excited about sharing the solemn awe and wonderment of this ancient shelter, this prehistoric womb, with Janette. Sadly, his excitement will be short-lived.

As they enter Paint Cave, Jamey again hears the words from The Book of Enoch. There is no explosion inside his brain this time, though. The words are manifested in the form of an ethereal Cherubic chant. I can hear the words too. This time it is not my doing.

Janette Dean hears nothing. Her world has become completely silent. The silence is so overwhelmingly ominous that her grip on reality, which had in fact begun evaporating several weeks ago, is now lost. Completely and irrevocably. She is looking but is not seeing. She is listening but is not hearing. She is talking but there are no words. Janette looks around for Jamey but he is not there. He has gone deeper into Paint Cave. His presence has been requested.

After a brief time, Janette departs the cave and is walking in the general direction of the truck. She doesn't know where she is headed because she doesn't know where she is anymore. Janette is thinking she is a precocious five year old; sitting at the breakfast table making "yucky coffee" with her father. She giggles. Then suddenly, she begins to cry. Janette wants her mommy now. She has a bug on her. More than one, actually. "Mommy, Mommy! There's a bug on me! Get it off, Mommy!" She stumbles among the loose rocks.

Jamey walks out of Paint Cave just as Janette Dean is falling to the ground. She is screaming. Her hands are flailing at something on her body. From this distance Jamey can see small dark shapes covering her. The shapes are moving, scurrying I guess you could call it. Of course, by now Jamey knows what the shapes are, but he refuses to accept it. Not until he asks God why. And not until he kills himself. Unfortunately, God will let him do neither.

Oh, how I wish I could intervene at this very moment. Change everything. Or make Jamey Maxwell forget everything. But I cannot. As they say in here in West Texas: *Cuando Dios no quiere, los ángeles no pueden.* The angels cannot grant that which God will not permit. If nothing else, I would kill him mercifully, but God will not let Jamey die. Not yet. Jamey Maxwell still has a few things left to do on this Earth.

By the time he reaches Janette's side, the vinegaroons have completely engulfed her. Hundreds of vinegaroons. Their pedipalps gnashing. Their thin tails whipping from back to front, slinging acetic acid from their anal glands directly toward her eyes, with amazing accuracy (vinegaroons — very strange creatures — and their purpose? — more evidence of that "God works in mysterious ways" crap). Even with her eyes closed, the acid penetrates. Janette is screaming in pain — and terror. Taz, the mysterious dog-thing, is there too. I did not see him until now. Taz is watching curiously; *y con mucho más que tristeza.*

With both hands, Jamey lashes out at the vinegaroons, brushing as many as he can from Janette's body. He is trying to save her. This is a hopeless task for she is Nephilim and at God's disposal. There will be no mercy for Janette Dean. After several agonizing minutes, she falls silent and still. The whipscorpions disperse within a matter of seconds, as if they were an ephemeral nightmare. Jamey knows better. He might be crazy but he is not oblivious, no matter how much he wishes he was. He slowly walks back to his old blue pickup. Taz follows. Always watching. Always.

Janette Dean, five months pregnant, lies unconscious. Jamey Maxwell returns to her side muttering to God about unjustifiable punishment for the blameless.

Jamey is reprimanding God for His arbitrary and capricious judgments. Couldn't He be wrong, just this once? Jamey asks, but refuses to plead, to be absolved of his responsibility. God's answer comes swiftly. Jamey slowly raises his Smith and Wesson Model 59. The trigger is pulled.

In a back alley in St. Petersburg, Russia, a petty thief in the process of robbing an elderly man in the early stages of Alzheimer's disease, glances over his shoulder and shudders.

In a small village in Rwanda, on a filthy cot in a hut made of cow manure, a young AIDS victim, whose parents believe she is already dead, opens her jaundiced eyes wide and grins the most grotesque yellow grin.

In the Gaza Strip, in a crowded refugee camp, a master bomb maker, hesitates briefly before installing a detonator on his latest masterpiece.

In Buenos Aires, Argentina, a wealthy, but aging banker nearing orgasm with one of his favorite mistresses stops in mid-stroke.

In a remote mountain encampment in western Mongolia, a shepherd experiences a brief flash; a vision: his five-year-old son will die soon.

And in the West Texas town of Alpine, an elderly couple, Sam and Lilly Barden, owner of a non-descript junk yard on the outskirts of town, turn to each other and smile.

Taz, the blue heeler hybrid, lies down beside the body of Janette Dean, places his head on his front paws and his moist eyes become just a bit moister.

In Dos Cruces, Texas, in a small adobe workshop,

Daniel Galvan, the goatboy, dozes fitfully in an old hardwood chair. And Miguel Veras runs his increasingly arthritic hands up and down the carving of *La Virgen de Guadalupe.* For the first time in more than fifty years, the *santero* has missed something. Under the Virgin Mary's left breast is an aberration; an anomaly. In the exquisitely carved mesquite statue, Miguel's failing eyesight and ever more insensitive fingers have failed to detect the smallest of flaws.

Epilogue

Epilogue

Now the truth: my name is Azazel and I have lied to you. Don't say I did not warn you. No, I did not lie to you about the murders, the ensuing revenge killings, or any of those details. They are all so inconsequential. I lied to you about me.

I was once God's favorite. That was so long ago. *Hace muchos años*. The voice inside Jamey Maxwell's head all these years was not God's, it was mine. I needed him to do what I could not. Eliminate the Nephilim. And now they have been eliminated. Janette Dean was the last. Shall we recap? Janette Dean: Nephilim. Jacinto Ocala: Nephilim. Luther Axelrod, Dwayne Dubois, Bradley and Vanessa Scofield: deserved to die. Billy and Kristin Garnett, Angelita Cavazos, Marisol Cortinas, and, of course, Connie Lee, Julie and Josie Maxwell: innocent bystanders. Or what you humans euphemistically refer to as collateral damage. What can I say? War is hell. But for whatever it's worth, I did, and still do, love Jamey Maxwell. I suspect it is not reciprocal. Oh yes, what about little Ellie? And her unborn sibling? They, of course, were also Nephilim. It seems they didn't choose their parents well. Kind of like me, I guess. I will get to that in a moment.

You probably think there would be many Nephilim left after all these years, but as usual, you would be wrong. Jamey Maxwell was not my only protege. He was not my only Nephilim exterminator. I have had many. Including the Ultimate Exterminator. God, however, got tired of this project long ago. He has been so distracted for so long. But while He was focused, He did one hell of a job. By the time I got involved, there were not that many Nephilim left. Of the humans I have employed, Jamey Maxwell was the best. The very best. I think I will miss him.

You are no doubt curious to know how long I've been mentoring my prize student, Jamey Maxwell. Well, let's just say that I was there on his ninth birthday when the "shit-eating, mother-fucking" Goehlke brothers had their way with him. Afterwards, Jamey made his no-loopholes deal with God. The one where he suffers for all of his sins on Earth so he won't have to go to Hell. I didn't have the heart to tell him that agreement is moot, since it was me he was talking to, not God.

Actually, I have been with Jamey since his unfortunate birth. And to be honest, I think I was the one most thankful for his creation. I have always thought that at least one of us should benefit from his existence. We have been close for a long, long time. I have been with him through thick and thin, as you humans like to say. During the good times, we did not talk much — no need. But during the bad times, the inconsolable losses, the years of sorrow, like that tragic accident with his wife and daughters, I have always been there for him. Whispering encouragement in his ear. Do you realize how difficult it is to make an ordinary human being mad enough or crazy enough to kill another human being?

After the deaths of Janette Dean and her unborn child, Jamey Maxwell called his new friend, Luis Moya. He asked Luis to come to Paint Cave alone. Luis obliged. Luis was shocked when he arrived and had trouble comprehending what he was seeing. And what Jamey Maxwell was telling him. Jamey Maxwell appeared to be incoherent, but he wasn't. He was speaking Aramaic. He was speaking of The Book of Enoch, of the Nephilim, and about a God without mercy. Gradually, Jamey Maxwell became quiet. Then he became catatonic.

Oh yes, all of that immaculate planning that Vanessa Scofield put into the murders of Billy and Kristin Garnett? Well, I must take most of the credit for it. It's not that Vanessa Scofield would not have been a perfectly capable murderer on her own, but I needed it to be done just the right way. I needed her to place the bodies in just the right place. The vinegaroons, you see. I needed the vinegaroons. Jamey Maxwell needed the vinegaroons. Nephilim are vinegaroon magnets. Those who are intimately — and intimacy can mean many things — exposed to Nephilim are vinegaroon magnets. The difference is this: if a person has only been exposed to Nephilim, whipscorpions will engulf the victim, scurrying over the body, either dead or alive, searching for a soul. Once a soul is found, the whipscorpions disperse, doing no harm.

Even in death, the aura of Nephilim exposure attracts the vinegaroons. As was the case of Kristin Garnett. The vinegaroons that the young shepherd saw were scuttling only over Kristin's body, because of her "intimate exposure" to Dr. Janette Dean, psychiatrist. Because the bodies of her and her husband, Billy, were left intertwined, Manuelito thought they were covering both bodies. They weren't. Trust me.

If the person is Nephilim, the whipscorpions will continue the attack, sensing a lack of a soul, and unleash mass quantities of acetic acid into the Nephilim's eyes. The acetic acid does not kill them, of course. The shock does. And, if not the shock, other measures are required. God so works in mysterious ways.

And before you ask, Jamey Maxwell has vinegaroon immunity. I can do some voodoo too.

Little Ellie was euthanized by her mother two days before Janette Dean was destroyed. Dr. Dean, in her final days, became increasingly depressed. She was able to hide it from almost everyone. She came to believe that Ellie was destined for a life of misery. She came to believe that as Ellie's mother, and as a psychiatrist, she was no longer able to help her daughter; unable to protect her from the world. She came to believe that if she went into Ellie's room while her precious and precocious daughter was asleep, she could place a pillow gently over her little face and end all of her suffering. Dr. Dean felt good about this decision. She planned to follow this act of mercy with another act of mercy: her own suicide, which would of course save her unborn child from a life of pain. But there is something different about the Nephilim. They have an innate, probably God-given, affinity for life. An intrinsic knowledge that this is it for them. No hereafter, here after. God damned them from the beginning for their defectiveness: their lack of souls. However, I cannot get over this feeling that, just for the hell of it, He gave them an indelible desire to live. At all costs. Dr. Dean discovered that after killing her beautiful daughter, she did not have the guts to kill herself. *No hay problema.* That is why Jamey Maxwell was put on this Earth.

About now, officers from the San Antonio Police Department are searching the townhouse at 11901 Roosevelt Drive. They are not sure what they are looking for, but they detect that rather peppery smell that precedes the overwhelming stench of death. On the second floor, in a child's bedroom, they will find Ellie Dean lying in her bed, propped up comfortably on her pillow, holding her favorite stuffed animal, a silly-looking giraffe. Sadly, Ellie will be in a rapidly advancing state of decomposition. Unjustly, Jamey Maxwell will also be blamed for this murder. Life, especially human life, is so unfair.

Jamey Maxwell is directly or indirectly responsible for the deaths of six people on earth: Janette Dean, Brad and Vanessa Scofield, Luther Axelrod, Dwayne Dubois, and Jacinto Ocala. Each of them either a murderer or an accomplice to murder. And two of them Nephilim. You would think he would be treated as a hero, but I fear he will be treated more like a totally insane mass-murderer. As I said, life is unfair.

And, there is the dilemma of Janette Dean's unborn child — a fetus, if you will — who would have also been Nephilim.

Remember our discussion about "sex equals destruction?" Thank God, literally, that Angels are created in purity. No disgusting Angel fetuses. Does killing a five month old fetus constitute murder in the eyes of the law? If so, then I guess Jamey Maxwell will be called, among other things, a baby killer. But in God's eyes, the fetus was Nephilim and doomed to destruction. The law of man pales before God's. Remember, He sentenced me to be buried for eternity. That's a long time.

Jimmy Boyer, Jamey's old lawyer friend, will represent Jamey once again on murder charges. But this time, the brilliant attorney will not be able to exonerate his client. He will only be able to save his life with a successful, and obvious, insanity plea.

Oh, and one more minor detail: Jamey Maxwell did not pull the trigger. He would not. Could not. More human than I thought. I am not going to tell you he did not have the *cojones* to do it. I am going to tell you he had the *cojones* not to do it.

To be a little more specific, Jamey Maxwell, my bestest friend in the whole wide world, raised his little gun; then he held it to his head. I could not let him hurt himself though, could I? That's what friends are for, right? I saved his life. His miserable, motherfuckin' life. But, of course, Dr. Janette Dean had to go. So I did it. Oh yeah, I grew *grandes cojones* and did "the deed" big time. Not without dire consequences though. At the moment I pulled the trigger I became of this Earth. I knew that would happen. God does not let Watchers "join in all the reindeer games." We can talk and hint;

cajole and encourage. But to take physical action against humans, Watchers must become human. New rule God put in place after that little escapade in which I and two hundred of *mis cuñados* participated, oh so long ago. The one where we fucked female humans till the cows came home. More accurately, I have become psuedo-human. I like to think super human.

I made the choice. Free will? Angels have that too. God likes giving all His creations options. This time the consequence of my choice is permanent, but not infinite. I am here on Earth and now I will die here on Earth, eventually. Kind of like Jesus Christ. We both will have made sacrifices. He chose death over the eternal damnation of mankind. I have chosen death over eternal boredom. I will not die any time soon, I pray. But I will die.

Jamey Maxwell does not know any of this. He thinks he killed Janette Dean and her unborn fetus. By the way, it was a fetus *con* fetus in fetu. A Nephilim inside a Nephilim inside a Nephilim. I am sure you would like to tell Jamey Maxwell this. Give him the scoop and all that jazz. It won't do no fuckin' good. He don't hear too *bien* now. *No comprende* if you get my fuckin' drift.

But now, more about me. For eons virtually without end I was entombed, interred, buried alive. It was God's doing. Enoch was right about that. When time was new, after my little escapade with those human hussies, I was declared *angela non grata*. I was thrown to earth at Dudael which just happens to be in what you humans call West Texas. As God commanded, Raphael covered me with rough and jagged rocks. Since we Seraphs are infinite beings, I would have been there *todo el tiempo*. Forever. So, I guess I have lied to you about being many places over many millenia. However, I have done my research and I felt like I was there. Plus, Watchers share our institutional memory. Communicating through those unbelievably boring intuitive fucking vibrations. No more of that shit for me though. I'm human now — gonna talk the talk and walk the walk. Man, it feels so fucking good. I am alive!

In 1925, thanks to mankind, I was released. It was a tragedy for some, and deliverance for me. I doubt this was God's doing. On February 22, 1925, one mile west of Langtry, there was a tremendous explosion at the Southern Pacific Railroad rock quarry. Near the steam-driven rock crusher, "powder monkeys" had placed dynamite in almost fifty holes on the west side of the quarry. They were preparing to slice off a large portion of the steep limestone walls. This would provide large rocks for the crusher. Once crushed, the limestone was to be used as ballast to hold railroad ties in place. But something dreadful happened that day. And something wonderful. Premature detonation, I suppose. Eight men were killed — and an Angel was reborn.

And why did I need to eliminate the Nephilim, my offspring? For the same reason God tried to eliminate them, and thought He had, with the Great Flood. Because I was afraid they would corrupt the bloodline of the coming Messiah. And I am not speaking of the one God is sending.

When I came to earth the first time I made a mistake: I brought two hundred of my closest friends: Samlazaz, Araklba, Rameel, Sariel, and the rest. They no longer exist. I have told you Angels live forever, but there is an exception. God can destroy us if He so chooses. And in the case of my aforementioned cohorts, He chose to do just that. Since He perceived me to be the ringleader, and rightly so, He chose to bury me forever. To deprive me of light, His light. A punishment infinitely greater than non-existence. And since so much time had passed here on Earth, I had no way of knowing which of the Nephilim was of my seed. And I want, I need, purity. So I had no option but to destroy all that was left. Now I can start anew. Isn't that exciting? I can stay on this Earth for a while longer. I love it here. I think I can be a superstar. Of course, I'll have to metamorphize into the male of the human species. To propagate, I mean. Did you know that the Greeks liked to call Angels who came to Earth in human form, *sarkos heteras*? *Sarkos heteras*, strange flesh. Now that has a ring to it. Sounds like a wonderful name for an alternative rock band, doesn't it?

But what I would most like to tell you is that I am tired of being a scapegoat. Do you realize my name means "scapegoat?" It is formed from the Hebrew *'ez'* meaning 'goat' and *'azal'* meaning 'to go away'. Did you know the term was coined specifically for me? Did you know the holiest of Yahweh's solemn feast days, The Day of Atonement, is specifically about me? On the tenth day of the seventh month of Yahweh's Scriptural calendar, the high priest, Aaron, was to make an atonement for the sins of Israel. To accomplish this Aaron selected two young goats from the congregation of the children of Israel. He was then instructed to cast lots to determine which goat would be "for Yahweh" and which for "the scapegoat"...me. How does this make me feel? Mixed emotions, I guess. On the one hand, it makes me feel incredibly significant. On the other hand, why should I get blamed for all of the sins of the world? Just because I was — am — sexually attracted to human females? Then why not spread the blame around a bit? Say to three billion human males, and a hundred million human females.

Have you ever been unloved? Has Someone ever loved you so much that you started loving Them...and then They stopped loving you? Unloved: to us Angels, that is the definition of Hell.

I have loved twice. They were both mistakes. The first was my God. Your God. It has not turned out well. I tried. I tried hard for a long, long time. But he expects perfection and nothing less. At least for us Seraphs. And the other choirs too, but that is their problem. They will have to do the best they can. You humans, now that is a different story. God forgives you and forgives you until it makes me want to puke, if only we angels could. I am over all that now. It is a literally moot point.

But God was not my true love. There was another. To keep this in terms you humans can comprehend, I will call my lost love "her." I will give her a name, just to humor you. Her name was Iole. She too was a Seraph. She turned me on. Like a radio. Since we can appear to be whatever we choose, it sounds silly to say she was beautiful. Maybe it was because she chose to be someone I thought was beautiful that made me love her. I think it was more than that though. Actually, I know it was more than that. God made the same mistake twice too. Yes, I am keeping score. Somehow he gave two Seraphs human genes. Maybe it was not a mistake. Maybe it was some sort of sick experiment.

Whatever it was, she managed to finagle a special reward from the Big Guy. It will sound like punishment to you humans. As I've said several times, ya'll don't have a fucking clue. Her reward? She got to come to Earth as a human. Sounds like the opposite end of the spectrum from Enoch going directly to Heaven. Not really, though. Heaven had become Hell for Iole. Earth looked like Heaven.

The really good news is: I know where she lives. Alpine-fucking-Texas. She is number one on my visitor's list — with a bullet. I have a bone to pick with her. And, if she is lucky, I may give her a bone to chew. Man oh man, I am going to love being a man.

And remember my admonition about the one mortal sin in God's eyes? Presumptuousness? Well, that part is true. My, oh my, how man fucking presumes. Jamey Maxwell presumed God's will was to destroy all these people. In hindsight, how wrong was that? But, I have a feeling God will make an exception for him since it was all my doing. Free will was not really an option for Jamey Maxwell. So don't worry too much about his fate. I am sure I will reap the punishment for his sins. And for mine too. Later, not sooner, I pray. Does God know that I have escaped? Probably. Who knows? You say it's been seventy-seven years since I was reborn? Do you think that is a long time? Divide 15 billion into 77 and you will get your answer. It is less than the wink of God's enigmatic eye. And He has been so busy over these last seventy-seven years. Wars and rumors of war. Atrocities and rumors of atrocities. So I hope God is too distracted at present to trifle with me, because I have so much business to tend. But if He is not, what is the worst that can happen? I will be destroyed? *No le hace*. No pain, no suffering, no more coveting. Only blessed fucking nothingness. I can handle that.

One last thing: do you recall our little chat about man's narcissistically perceived role in the universe? And remember I alluded to a secret that man has yet to uncover? Maybe the universe isn't so empty after all. Maybe God liked His little experiment on Earth so much that He replicated it billions and billions of times throughout the cosmos. And there are millions and millions of planets much larger than earth. Some that can hold a hundred billion humans. Yes, I said humans. Seems that God went over the edge with His special creations. He loved humans so much He didn't know when to stop. Pandora's Box became Pandora's Wide Open Beaver. And, now maybe there are Messiahs "coming soon to a galaxy near you." Millions, make that billions, of them, in fact. So I doubt He cares if the Messiah coming to Earth, this puny pointless planet, is His…or mine. We will see. We will see.

Hope and Dreams

Jamey Maxwell is five years old. He is sitting on the concrete sidewalk, in his little white undies, bouncing a red rubber ball up against the cement steps. Catching it as it ricochets. Bouncing and catching. Bouncing and catching. His daughters, Julie and Josie are sitting next to him. He catches the ball, turns to them, smiles and says, "It's okay now. I know what to do." Jamey Maxwell continues bouncing and catching. He is still smiling. So is Alphonso.

A preview of the first three chapters of

Stalking Azazel

VOLUME THREE OF THE DOS CRUCES TRILOGY

by

James A. Mangum

Prologue

Jamey Maxwell remembers driving by a Church of Christ in Ft. Worth many years ago. The sign in front of the church said this: HELL IS REAL. At the time, he chuckled to himself, "Well that's a great thought to start the day." In his mind now the sign appears. This time, he does not chuckle. Jamey Maxwell is catatonic.

Part I

Hell is Real: (The Escape)

Chapter 1

Catatonia

Catatonia-(n) a form of schizophrenia characterized by a tendency to remain in a fixed stuporous state for long periods; the catatonia may give way to short periods of extreme excitement.

The most dangerous criminals in Texas do not reside at the Polunsky Unit in Huntsville, Texas, more famously known as Death Row. They reside at the Skyview Psychiatric Unit in Rusk, Texas. Jamey Maxwell is among them now.

My name is Alphonso and I look after him. As much as an orderly can look after a completely insane, catatonic, mass murderer. In my case, that's quite a bit. I have been assigned to Jamey Maxwell by the head of this hospital and by the Head of the universe. I am a black man and I am an angel.

My job as an orderly is to keep Jamey from killing himself. My job as an angel is to explain his life to him; how he has been manipulated. Also, my job is to help him escape and begin his final job on Earth. Track down and kill the angel Azazel who is now of the Earth. Azazel is bipolar, psychotic, and psychopathic.

And he has serious issues. In his current incarnation as a man, Azazel seeks a suitable woman with whom to mate. He wants a son…or daughter. He is not choosey about this. Either one will become the new Messiah. *Sarkos heteros*, strange flesh, is what the ancient Greeks would have called Azazel once he descended to Earth as a man. God calls him an abomination.

I am assigned to Ward D, second floor. I am responsible for seven very crazy humans. Only one will be cured.

Jamey Maxwell is in no condition to hear all of this just yet. He will be soon. I will slowly bring him out of his state of catatonia — into a new state — paranoia. It is a process. It is required.

Chapter 2

Paranoia

Paranoia- (n) a psychotic disorder characterized by delusions of persecution with or without grandeur, often strenuously defended with apparent logic and reason.

More than a prison hospital, more than a building even, the Skyview Psychiatric Unit is a vessel. The vessel is full. Full of pain, full of rage, full of hate, full of loneliness, full of insanity. But is also a vessel full of strange love, full of sweet twisted dreams which will never be fulfilled, full of faux hopes which have no names. The Skyview Psychiatric Unit is a vestigial vessel: full of everything good that is left in man. It is a malignant vessel: full of everything bad that has evolved in man. It is the remains of what began in the Garden eons ago. It is a monument to God's good plan gone awry.

"Hey, bro, whatcha know?" This has been my greeting to Jamey Maxwell each day for the last year and three months. Each day I have received a blank stare as a reply. Today is different. Today Jamey Maxwell is looking at me. Now he is smiling. Now he is crying.

Not a loud cry, just tears streaming down his face.

Jamey Maxwell is conflicted. Now that he realizes he is still alive, his primitive brain is telling him he should be happy. His highly developed, psychically damaged brain tells him otherwise. I will soon tell him how precious life is, but not for the reason most humans think.

Jamey is still unable to talk. That is fine. For now, I just need him to listen. Jamey has been tricked, duped, swindled, bamboozled, for his entire life. By Azazel. Jamey always thought it was God talking to him. But it was Azazel all along. Azazel, the cosmic ventriloquist; the talented abomination; the god of liars.

I begin: "You know, bro, it ain't your doin'. It ain't what you think. You been ridin' the Azazel train. No control. It ain't God that told you all that bullshit. It was Azazel. He a motherfucker. So, what we gonna do about it? We gonna kick his fuckin' ass…." And I go on. And on. Through the night I explain how things have transpired in Jamey Maxwell's life. How he never had a chance. How he was taken hostage as a child. How none of this was his fault. How he must seek and exact revenge. I speak in the vernacular of a black man in the Texas prison system. People are always close at hand, listening here. Not so much to the content of what another says, but the inflections and intonations. And always the obscenities. It is required. Anyway, as long as I speak calmly no one actually hears the words. Except for Jamey Maxwell, of course.

The paranoia is setting in. I can see it in Jamey's eyes. And who is to blame him? Considering all he has been through the past few years. The damage that

Azazel has done to him is permanent; strong. It will take all my strength as an angel to overcome this. If you were Jamey Maxwell, would you believe me? I did not think so.

I must bring him along slowly. I could lose him still. He could shatter at any time. So here goes. Jamey knows this is not hypnosis for he could not possibly be hypnotized. He senses there is a name for this, but the name became extinct light years ago. He is talking to his beloved Connie Lee now. I am giving him a rare opportunity; the chance to ask for retroactive forgiveness. He has forgotten that she and his daughters are dead.

Chapter 3

Schizophrenia

Schizophrenia-(n) a severe mental disorder characterized by psychotic symptoms — thought disorder, hallucinations, delusions, paranoia — and impairment in job and social functioning.

His name is Stephen and he is a black man like me. Stephen is twenty-four years old, chronologically. Seven years old mentally. Seventy years old spiritually. He is morbidly obese. He is sweet. Seven years ago he killed his mother and stepfather. Then he spent days mutilating them; just like he has done to himself since he was seven years old. Self-mutilation is relatively common here at Skyview. Most of the men do it out of boredom. Stephen does it out of disgust for himself.

The first thing he did after killing his stepfather was cut off the dead man's penis with a butcher knife. Stephen felt instant relief. He took the severed penis out into the back yard and buried it. He cried. Then he went back inside and began the process of incising various body parts on both his mother and stepfather. Intricate, fantasy designs embellished with a few words: 'love'; 'unicorn'; 'happy'; 'momma'; 'heaven'. The detectives spent time trying to decipher the message, but after a while concluded there was none. Of course, there was. But it was a message only Stephen and God understood.

Stephen continues to mutilate himself here at Skyview despite the best efforts of the staff to keep all sharp objects away from him. Where there's a will, there's a way, as you humans like to say. The eating utensils are plastic and make nice jagged edges when you break them. As do toothbrushes. Stephen spends a lot of time in the infirmary. His personal hygiene is poor so Stephen suffers from a variety of infections. Of course his counselor talks to Stephen about all this weekly. Stephen always promises to stop cutting himself. Stephen likes to tell everyone what they want to hear. He used to do that with his stepfather.

The staff gives Stephen crayons. He draws the most wonderful fantasy pictures. There is already a blossoming trade in Stephen Bowen drawings among the prison staff. And now, in the art world. Stephen is totally unaware of this. Some of his drawings have sold for as much as $400 on eBay. Stephen is becoming a hot commodity. And if he knew this it would mean about as much to him as it would to almost any seven year old.

As he walks by me I say, "How's it goin' my man?"

"Fine, Mr. A. I made a new drawing today. It's a dragon. It's red," Stephen replies.

"I'd like to see it, Stephen," I say, knowing it's already been scarfed up.

"I gave it to Randy. He said he likes dragons. He

said it was pretty good."

Randy Owens, a redneck, bigoted, lying, thieving, motherfucking, cocksucking prison guard. Pardon my French. Most Watchers, as myself, have become enamored of human languages. For some reason, we seem partial to curse words. Perhaps it is contrast we are seeking. I suspect there will be justice in this world for Randy Owens. I know there will be justice for him in the world after this one.

About the Author

James A. Mangum was born and raised in South Texas. He has lived and worked throughout the United States for the federal government as a Sky Marshal and Special Agent with the U.S. Treasury Department, a Federal Game Warden, an Investigator with the Office of Federal Investigations, and a Civil Rights Manager. He has been a co-owner of an oil and gas business and has most recently moved to Shiner, Texas, "the cleanest little city in Texas," where he now works as a folk artist, rescuer of wayward homes, and a teller of tales.